I0603814

VALERIE MASSEY GOREE

Every Hidden Thing

Valerie Massey Goree

What Readers are Saying

Shadows of Time:

"Read. This. Book. Even if contemporary or romantic suspense fiction isn't normally your "thing" you'll love this book. The plot line is a fascinating what if scenario that seems chillingly possible. I love that author tied the story to the past, and real historical events are referenced, adding more credibility to the plot. The story opens with a bang and kept me turning pages to the very end. There are twists and turns that add depth and intrigue. The author obviously did her research, and I can't imagine how much study it took to become knowledgeable enough to write the book. The topic of genetics is deeply scientific, but the author wove the information into the book mostly through snippets of dialog, so I was able to understand without having to look up stuff or feel like I was reading a textbook. The book is set in the Seattle area, and the description helped me visual the surroundings, giving me a virtual visit. The characters are well-written, and I especially love Cullen, flawed, yet likable, with an unusual set of traits. Highly recommended."

*Best-selling author, Linda Shenton Matchett.

"***Forever Under Blue Skies*** made me want to visit Australia. The two mysteries woven into the story kept me turning the pages and the proposal was so romantic, I had to read it twice."

*Amazon Reader Review

Other Books By Valerie Massey Goree
Texas Suspense:
Deceive Me Once
Colors of Deceit

Stolen Lives Trilogy:
Weep in the Night
Day of Reckoning
Justice at Dawn

Stand Alone:
Forever Under Blue Skies

My Mother's Secret:
Shadows of Time

Trigger: One of the topics discussed in this book is miscarriage.

"For God will bring every deed into judgment, including
every hidden thing, whether it is good or evil."
Ecclesiastes 12:14 (NIV)

Chapter 1

Tremaine Realty specialized in prime waterfront properties on the Pacific Northwest's Olympic and Kitsap Peninsulas. As a junior agent and a nepotism-hire, instead of only showing fancy homes to prospective clients, Joanna Tremaine was more often than not assigned to the property management division of the company. Like today. But she had no grounds to complain. In reality, she considered this a choice assignment. She loved the prospect of fixing up something broken and making it presentable again, and since her folks had given her a job after her interior design business went belly-up, she was determined to prove worthy of their trust.

The serious GPS voice announced her destination ahead, Nelda Yates's extensive property south of Seabeck on the Hood Canal side of the Kitsap Peninsula. Jo stopped at the open electric gate. *Item number one on the repair list: Fix gate.* She drove up the paved, curved driveway shaded by ancient firs and gawked at the stone mansion appearing through the branches. What a house! But when Jo parked in front of the three-car garage, the neglect became apparent. Cracked windows, peeling paint on the wood trim, weeds forcing their way between pavers. No wonder Nelda hired Tremaine Realty to prepare the property for sale.

Purse and briefcase in hand, Jo removed the key from the lock box. The carved oak door swung open into a cathedral-ceilinged foyer. "Wow." Jo pivoted slowly, taking in the grandeur. Eager to begin documenting needed touch-ups and repairs, she sauntered through the massive living room where sunlight poured in through floor-to-ceiling windows, then entered the kitchen at the rear. Her mouth gaped. The room was large enough to accommodate her whole apartment. She dumped her purse and briefcase onto the counter.

The only distraction came from the overflowing trashcan beside the refrigerator. Sour milk topped the rank odors. Jo tamped down the contents with her booted foot and closed the lid.

iPad ready, she opened the back door. She preferred completing the outdoor phase first and ventured to the weathered barn about one hundred yards from the house. The doors hung like loose teeth. Foul, dank air engulfed her. Decaying animal waste carpeted the ground. She wrinkled her nose and stepped carefully. *Mama, this is why I wear boots.* Jo snickered. She always had to defend her choice of wardrobe to her dainty, immaculate mother.

Jo took a dozen or more photos of the dilapidated barn. She would recommend its removal. Satisfied she'd captured all the outside details, she stepped to the door.

The matted straw to her left rustled.

Rodents? Ugh.

A dog whined and poked his dirty head through the stubble. "You poor thing." Jo leaned over, but he withdrew. "I won't hurt you." She used a rake handle to move the straw and gasped. The mid-sized dog was entwined in a coil of barbed wire. He cowered, making it difficult for Jo to extricate him, but one last twist, and he was free. The pooch, with only minor scrapes, scampered away, scruffy brown tail between his legs.

Jo picked up the wire and frowned. In his struggles, the dog had rumpled a dirty, khaki tarpaulin which partially covered a metal container. In order to read the red lettering, she picked up a corner of the canvas and gulped.

DANGER; EXPLOSIVES.

Taking a step backward, she stared at her discovery. Surely the former tenants hadn't left dynamite behind. Aware she'd have to notify the authorities, Jo threw back the tarpaulin to see what else it might conceal and exposed two more green, metal containers. Each measured about fifteen-by-twelve-by-six inches and had handles on the sides.

Had the renters used the barn to store other

hazardous items? Jo noted marks in the dirt floor which could indicate heavy objects had been dragged along. And the path to the—

Strident, angry voices floated into the barn through gaps in the wooden slats.

Jo covered the containers, then peeked out through a large gap and spied two people walking from the tree line at the end of the property toward the barn.

"You didn't have to come. Don't you trust me?" Male, wearing blue jeans and a tan T-shirt.

"No, I don't, Wade." Female in maroon pants and jacket. "It was your responsibility to load all the ammo containers."

Not dynamite, but ammunition. Jo headed to the door but stopped when the female continued her harangue in a venomous tone.

"Were you planning on coming back for them later to sell yourself?" She tugged at a pale scarf around her neck.

"No. How could you think that, Rosie? I promise, I just forgot how many containers we had."

Their voices grew louder as they neared Jo's position.

"You've put us all in danger. If they fall into the wrong hands, our whole organization could be jeopardized."

"It's not my fault we had to leave in such a hurry. Besides, who's going to find them way out here?" Wade stomped ahead of his companion.

Aha. The previous tenants.

"Of all the stupid—"

A cell phone rang. The pair halted, not three yards from Jo. Rosie withdrew a phone from her jacket pocket. "It's Boyd. I'll put it on speaker. Yeah?"

"Keep your voices down." Another male. "I think someone's in the house."

"What?" Rosie and Wade hissed together.

"I just drove past and noticed a vehicle in the driveway. Have you collected the merchandise?"

Jo shot a quick glance at the tarpaulin. Considering the theme of the conversation, she had no doubt that revealing her presence would not be healthy.

"No." Rosie jabbed Wade's shoulder. "We haven't entered the barn yet."

"Get out of there, sis, and don't return. I'll wait until the person leaves, then I'll pick up the containers."

Wade grabbed Rosie's arm as she ended the call. "Why did you narc on me to Boyd?"

"I had to. Although he's my brother, he wouldn't have given me any slack if I hadn't. Let go. You're hurting me."

He did not release her. "Oh, no. I forgot—"

"What?"

"Molly's box of little toys."

Rosie wrenched her arm free and pounded on Wade's chest. "You stupid man. Why did I ever marry you?"

"Quit." He deflected her next assault. "Boyd can get

it. We gotta go."

As the intruders ran across the lawn, Rosie's scarf floated to the ground. She stopped and retrieved it, then the couple disappeared into the woods.

Slumping against the wall, Jo rubbed her forehead. Close call. It seemed obvious their possession of ammo containers was suspicious. After one last peek through the gap, Jo hightailed it back to the house and made sure all the doors were locked. Although the locks had been changed over the weekend, she couldn't risk a surprise visit from Boyd.

Hand shaking, Jo removed her phone from her pocket and called the Kitsap County

Sheriff's Office. A deputy in the area would arrive as soon as she tended to a minor fender-bender. To calm her jittery insides, Jo sat in the bay window seat in the kitchen and sipped from her water bottle. Her gaze wandered around the room and she fantasized about changes she'd make. Replace the gaudy backsplash with neutral-colored tiles. Stainless steel appliances instead of black. She sighed. Rented apartments were all she could afford for now.

Composure restored, Jo returned to her task photographing and itemizing needed repairs of the downstairs rooms. Patch up a couple of scrapes and paint the walls, change out mismatched light fixtures. Update the drab half-bathroom. Other than a thorough cleaning, not much else required attention.

However, the upstairs rooms were a disaster. Jo

vowed to never rent out any home she might acquire in the future. Empty cardboard boxes and odd bits of furniture littered the three large bedrooms. Had Boyd also lived here? If so, he, Wade, and Rosie must have packed up in a hurry, but that didn't account for stained carpets, holes in the sheetrock, or chipped bathroom tiles. They would not be getting their security deposit returned, for sure. The previous property management company certainly failed in their responsibilities, especially in vetting the last tenants.

In the smallest bedroom, Jo found no damage at all. A tattered little stuffed bunny on the window sill indicate this might have been their child's room. She opened the closet and other than a missing lightbulb, all seemed in good order. In her limited experience, she'd noted that if tenants left anything behind it was usually something on the top shelf in a closet. At nearly six-feet tall, Jo had no need to stand on tiptoe to reach a shoebox stashed way back against the wall. The box Wade left behind? Jo was not surprised to find an assortment of little toys inside. The kind that might be included in a children's meal from a fast food restaurant. Molly must be pretty attached to the toys for Rosie to be so annoyed at her husband's forgetfulness. Jo took the box and would later contact the tenants.

After a half-hour of documenting the damage and the need to remove the awful, floral wallpaper in the three bathrooms, Jo descended the stairs and noted three cracked spindles. She added the repairs to her list and returned to the kitchen where she set the shoebox with her personal items. Next on her agenda—the dock and waterfront picnic area. She traipsed along the worn path that led down to the bay. Around a clump of potted bushes she spied a sturdy, almost new dock jutting into the water about ten feet, but no sign of tables or benches. New owners could furnish the area to suit themselves. She'd ask the landscapers to remove the large pots. Several were cracked and most of the plants were either dead or overgrown.

On her way back to the house, Jo puzzled over the well-used path. Interesting in that the dock looked as if it hadn't been used much. She checked the gardens, beginning with those around the front deck. Weed removal, add mulch and additional hydrangeas and salvia. Taking photos as she walked, she wandered down the driveway and noted landscape problems, especially the pruning or removal of rogue blackberry vines that dominated a hedge of colorful rhododendrons. Overhanging fir tree branches needed trimming, and the vast lawn had to be mowed and edged. She added the disconnected and lopsided electric gate to her list.

Noting a piece of trash in the shrubs, she squeezed between the thick bushes avoiding the blackberry thorns and nabbed the plastic bag. Footsteps crunched on the driveway. Wade or Rosie? Jo peeked through the leaves. Neither. A tall, muscular man walked down the middle of the drive, peering ahead.

Jo stepped forward. "Can I help you?"

The man halted, hand to his chest. "You startled me." He blew out a breath. "Good morning. I live in the area and I'm curious. Are you the new tenant?"

They were too far from the house for him to see the magnetic advertisement on her SUV. Jo extricated herself from the branches and extended her hand. "Jo Tremaine from Tremaine Realty."

"Um, Gerald. Gerry with a 'G'." He shook her hand then pointed over his shoulder. "Is the house for sale? Will you be the listing agent?"

"Yes. As soon as we have it in tiptop shape."

"Great. I'm glad you're here. The unkempt yard is an eyesore." The guy's dark brown eyes were in sharp contrast to his sandy-colored hair.

"We'll soon have it under control."

"I'll pass the word that the property will be on the market." He cocked his head. "You're taking pictures?"

"Yes." Jo held up her iPad. "To document damage and areas in need of attention."

"Did the tenants leave a mess?"

Strange question. "You could say that." He didn't need any more details. "I have a lot to do. Nice to meet you, Gerry."

"Same here. Sorry for taking up your time. Do you have a card so I can refer prospective clients?"

"Certainly." Jo drew the slim holder from her back pocket and handed him a card. "I appreciate any business you send my way."

"Thanks." He beamed a bright smile at her, then walked down the drive. His well-fitting dark slacks accentuated his long legs. At the gate, he turned and gave her a brief wave.

Jo nibbled her bottom lip and followed the driveway to the house. Interesting guy. A commanding physical presence, but he showed a lot of interest in the former renters. She halted. *I should have asked for his full name.* The authorities might want to question him. Well, if he lived in the neighborhood as he claimed, they'd probably meet him.

Although he'd given his name as Gerald and not Boyd, Jo's senses were on full alert, and she hurried to the front door. The rhododendron shrubs ahead rustled. She sucked in a breath. Not a snake. She hated snakes. The bottom leaves quivered and the same dog she'd seen in the barn emerged. This time, a long piece of fabric, which looked vaguely familiar, dangled from his mouth. When he noticed Jo, he dropped the rag and scurried away.

"Come back, puppy dog. I won't hurt you. I'll take you home with me." Still wary of the man she'd met, she hesitated to check on the dog's gift, but her conscience nagged at her. She'd recently seen something similar.

Using a stick, she snagged a corner of the flimsy cloth, and held it up. Rosie's floral scarf. Jo reached out to touch the material, but stopped. Some of the pink and purple flowers had an ivory background, while others were surrounded by crimson…that seemed to be spreading. With the stick at arm's length, her gaze traveled down the fabric. Red droplets splattered onto the pavers. Blood? "Little dog, what have you done?"

A powerful motor purred behind Jo. She turned.

The Kitsap County Sheriff parked her forest-green SUV next to Jo's vehicle.

Carrying the bloody scarf on the stick, Jo approached the deputy. "The situation has changed."

Chapter 2

Two more boxes to empty and he'd be done. Flynn McCaul wiped sweat off his forehead and dropped to the bed. Moving boxes of books from the living room to the second bedroom, which also served as his office, sapped his last ounce of strength. He massaged his aching left shoulder, careful to avoid the scars, then stared at his disfigured and shriveled left leg. The throbbing, tingling nerve pain was pronounced, probably from all the walking with heavy loads he'd done. Almost a decade of service in the US Marines with nary a scratch only to be injured a year later in the accident that killed his parents.

Flynn stood and shook off the memories. He removed books from the boxes and arranged them on shelves near his desk. Dozens of tomes that reflected his interest in the US Marines who served during both World Wars. Some were eyewitness accounts and had no glossy covers, but exuded the dusty smell of old paper. With the last book in place, he stepped back and nodded. Yup. Good idea to have them in here and not in the living room.

He flattened the boxes and carried them to the back door. As he reached for the knob, his cell phone rang. The boss, Thomas Tremaine. "Morning, sir." Flynn limped to the living room and sank onto his oversized russet-brown recliner.

"Call me Thomas, young man. I won't tell you again. Do you want me to order you to do pushups when next we meet?"

Flynn chuckled. "No, sir. Um, Thomas."

"How's the unpacking?"

"Done. Now I have to find a place for everything. Thanks for the day off to take care of business."

"You deserved it since you worked all weekend finalizing the training presentation. All set for tomorrow?"

"Yes, s…Thomas. It should take about ninety minutes, and I've arranged for lunch as well." Flynn bent his left leg and massaged his outer calf. Although the numbness persisted, therapists encouraged him to stimulate blood flow.

"Great. One bit of news. I contacted Joanna, and she is willing to make the swap with Wesley Isenberg. Maybe you can discuss the details with them tomorrow."

"No problem." After the call ended, Flynn stretched out, set his arms behind his head, and evaluated his recent job change. Although his response to Thomas had easily slipped out of his mouth, he was anything but sanguine about the idea of working with the boss's daughter. But even if he'd known about the possibility, he would have signed the contract anyway.

So far, the move to Tremaine Realty had proven beneficial. The opportunity to head the Silverdale office and use his tech knowledge to make improvements for the company, and to keep working part-time for his brother-in-law's construction business. All in all, a pretty good deal. Having Joanna in the same office couldn't be too bad. His fellow agents had nothing but positive opinions of her. The only negative comments came from Serena.

The very thought of the blonde sent Flynn's pulses running for cover and he straightened. Her classic features and athletic body caught his eye, but the suggestive vibes he picked up squelched any interest. And if only she knew how her snarky comments about Joanna detracted from her outward beauty. He fanned his face. Yeah. Without even meeting Joanna, he decided he'd rather work with her than Serena any day.

But the clincher to accepting the job had been Thomas's willingness to back Flynn's desire to find affordable living options for veterans. That alone made the move from Spokane worthwhile.

Grabbing his glass of orange juice from the side table, he drained it and smacked his lips, eyeing his surroundings. His condo was smaller than the one he'd left, but being on the ground floor in a complex without an elevator, meant he didn't have to contend with stairs.

He could navigate flat or inclined surfaces, but the brace he usually wore to support his dropped foot made climbing stairs difficult. Although Silverdale was about one-tenth the size of Spokane, the weather was much cooler, and that suited Flynn. He'd discovered over the years that hot temperatures exacerbated his nerve pain.

He eased out of the recliner and rearranged the orange and yellow cushions on the sofa. Not his choice of colors, but according to Melanie, his sister, he needed accessories to brightened up the beige tones of his living room. She was right. As usual. He sighed and picked up a stack of picture frames he wanted on the mantel. The first photo featured a trio of fellow Marines in fatigues. Edwards had been killed in Iraq in the same battle where Volcker lost an arm. Although Cole only received minor injuries during his service, he suffered from monumental Post Traumatic Stress. Couldn't hold a job. His wife divorced him. He resorted to drugs and alcohol for relief, had attempted suicide, and now lived on the streets.

Flynn set the frame on the mantel and hung his head. He knew of so many veterans in Cole's position. *Father God, please be with my buddies, especially Cole. Help them find comfort and support in You.*

Running a finger along the gilded frame, Flynn nodded. With Thomas's help, he had high hopes of turning his dream into reality. Housing and job opportunities for vets in need.

He set the next frame in place. The three McCaul

kids. Flynn, the tallest in the middle, Melanie, thirty-four, the eldest on his left, and Ian the youngest at twenty-nine, on his right. Good memories were shattered when he placed the next picture. Mom and Dad. The noise of the explosion ricocheted in Flynn's head. He backed away until his legs hit the sofa and he sank down.

Although an intruder had exacerbated the situation, Flynn took full responsibility for the accident. Events leading up to the nightmare were never far from his mind. He'd made the arrangements for the whole family to spend a long weekend near Cle Elum Lake in a remote cabin to celebrate their parents' thirty-fifth anniversary. The owner, a friend, Karl Mathis, reassured him the cabin was in perfect shape. But the pilot light for the old gas range did not work.

On their second day there, a burglar entered the house while the family had been at the lake. Flynn's parents returned to take a nap and the trespasser knocked Dad unconscious and forced Mother to locate valuables and cash. When Flynn heard a loud noise from the cabin, he ran up the hill to investigate. A noxious, sulphury odor hit him in the face as he entered the kitchen. Gas mixed with foul body odor.

He'd evaluated the scene in one sweep. Dad on the floor. Mother at the mercy of a hoodlum who held her in a headlock, knife to her throat. The thug had opened the oven door, and by the hissing, had turned on each burner. He held a utility lighter Karl kept beside the range. With a distorted expression on his face, he ranted at Mother for not getting him enough money and yelled for Flynn to stay back.

Unkempt clothing, bloodshot eyes, jittery movements. The man acted as if he needed a big-time fix. Flynn wasn't about to argue with him. Instead, he stared into Mother's eyes, willing her to recall self-defense lessons he'd given her. *Grab his arm. Grab and twist. Kick his shin.* Any of the numerous tactics he'd stressed for freeing herself from an assailant's hold. But Mother whimpered, her lower jaw quivering, and clawed at the man's arm.

Flynn had to act. He inched closer. The man took a step backward. Flynn was never sure what he intended, but the thief stumbled, flung his arm out and the utility lighter hit the range.

Boom. The range blew up, igniting the gas-filled kitchen, instantly killing his parents, the intruder, and wounding Flynn. He thanked the Lord every day the rest of the family had still been down at the lake when the explosion occurred.

Four years ago and the acrid smell of the smoke still lingered in his nostrils. The physical pain he'd experienced in his leg, torso, and shoulder could not compare to what he'd suffered at the sight of his parents' still bodies.

He drew in calming breaths. Over and over. In the quiet of his new home, he clutched the frame to his chest. When he'd arrived at the cabin and discovered the pilot light didn't work, he should have tried to clean out the pilot port. But he didn't. A decision that still haunted him. Sure, the addict could have blown out a functioning pilot light, but in his state of mind, Flynn figured the guy wouldn't have known to take that action. Authorities later confirmed the intruder had stolen from other cabins and camp sites.

And Mother? He should have stressed she practice the defensive moves he'd taught her months before when a friend of hers had been killed during a home invasion. But all the should-haves couldn't change the past.

Flynn rested against the colorful cushions and looked at the remaining two pictures. A family group taken last Christmas of Melanie and her husband, Stan, and their kids, eight-year-old Pam, and Haley, ten. His sister had forgiven him, and helped him as much as possible during his recovery and rehab. But Ian had not spoken to him since the accident. Flynn stood and set the pictures with the others. Ian in his dress blues, a smart Marine who resembled their father. Slim and trim, dark hair, and blue eyes.

Another reason Flynn opted to move from Spokane was to be closer to his siblings. Melanie lived in Edmonds, just north of Seattle, and Ian was presently stationed at Camp Pendleton in California with the Marine Expeditionary Force. One way or another, Flynn would reconcile with Ian even if it took the rest of his life.

Chapter 3

Fingerprints taken for elimination purposes. Questions answered. Descriptions given. Details repeated again and again. "Yes, Rosie wore the scarf. The phone call came from Boyd. Both Rosie and Wade had dark hair and were probably in their late twenties. Neither entered the barn. I didn't see Boyd."

Two hours after her discovery, the deputies allowed Jo to leave Nelda's house. As soon as Deputy Frances Gordon took possession of the bloody scarf, she'd called for back-up and had instructed Jo to wait on the front deck strewn with dried pine needles. When Deputy Zach Davis arrived, he'd searched the house and grounds while Gordon had continued to questioned Jo.

Concluding the interview, the deputy stood. "Thanks for your card, Miss Tremaine. We'll contact you if we need any additional information, and we'll let you know when you can return."

"What about the ammo and the blood? Is Rosie hurt?" Jo eased out of the chair. Didn't she deserve answers?

Gordon set her hands on her duty belt at her hips. "No comment at this time."

"Okay. May I collect my bags from the kitchen?"

"Go ahead. And don't forget to email us the tenant's details."

"I will. Do you need access to the house, or can I lock up?"

"We're done."

Jo tromped inside and gathered her purse, briefcase, and the shoebox. She noted the sheriffs had taken the bag of trash, but wrinkled her nose against the lingering odors. At the last minute, she looked in the refrigerator. No sense leaving items that might spoil before the cleaners arrived. Eggs, half-empty jelly jars, lunch meat, and a wilting carrot. Nothing that needed immediate removal.

Aha. The little dog would benefit from the lunch meat. In the back of a cabinet she found a dented meal bowl which she washed and filled with water, then she tore the meat into bits and piled them on a jar lid, also from the cabinet. Best not to wander too far from the house. Jo set the water and food on the back porch, locked the kitchen door, and carried her belongings to her car. After dumping all in the passenger seat, she locked the front door of the house and secured the key in the lockbox.

She gave the deputies a wave and reversed, but her phone rang before she headed down the driveway. Max.

What did he want?

"I thought we ended this relationship a week ago."

"Please, Jo. I want you to reconsider. I'm willing to admit I expected you to give up too much. Can we meet?"

The deep, bass tone of his voice conjured up his swarthy good looks and jovial personality. Jo rolled her eyes. *Stick to your decision.* "Sorry, Max. I shouldn't have to change my life to marry you. If you truly loved me, you'd accept me for who I am. Goodbye." She ended the call and threw her phone onto the passenger seat. It bounced off and landed on the floor. Grinding her teeth, she sped down the driveway and had to swerve close to the rhododendron bushes when a bomb squad vehicle entered from the street. Of course, the deputies wouldn't take Rosie's word the containers held ammunition. To calm her rapidly beating heart, Jo breathed deeply then turned right onto the road and passed several looky-loos. Gerry stood with the group and signaled her to stop. It would be rude to avoid him, so she complied.

He addressed her through her open window. "Are you all right? I noticed the sheriffs' cars, and now the bomb squad."

Willing her words to sound natural, Jo cleared her throat. "I'm fine, thanks." *Liar.*

"What's going on?" He rested his forearms on her window opening, glanced at the passenger seat then back at her.

Jo had no inclination to have a lengthy conversation with the man. Besides, she wasn't about to divulge what she'd found. "I'm not sure." Partial truth.

"Hey, if you don't mind me saying, your voice is shaky. You've had a shock."

"No, I haven't." She checked her reflection in the rearview mirror. Although she hadn't shed any tears over Max's call, her face was blotchy and her nose red. She giggled. "You got me. I did find something unusual at the house, and I, uh, received bad news."

"I know we've just met, but would you like to go for a cup of coffee or something to eat? There's a little place not far from here."

The sincerity in his voice and the intensity of his chocolate eyes nearly convinced her. "I could use a jolt of caffeine, but I need to get back to the office."

Gerry placed his hand on her arm, a warm comforting touch. "I understand. Take care, Miss Joanna. I hope to see you again."

She almost raised her foot off the brake pedal when she remembered the mutt. "Did the previous tenants have a dog?"

He shrugged. "I don't know. Why?"

"I saw a shaggy little brown dog cowering in the back yard."

"Maybe a stray. I'll keep an eye out." He jutted his chin toward her passenger seat. "I see the renters left shoes behind."

"Not exactly." Jo moved her briefcase to hide the

box. "Did you know the tenants?"

"No. I only noticed their vehicles coming and going and their lack of gardening skills."

"So you probably don't know where they moved to."

He hiked a shoulder and shook his head.

"Too bad. I'd like to return the box. Oh, well. I'm sure we have an email for them back at the office. Do you know how old their child was?"

"Uh, child? No." His face reddened and he crossed his arms. "I have your number and will call if I hear of anyone interested in the property."

"Thanks." Jo drove down the road, keeping an eye on Gerry in the rearview mirror. She'd almost agreed to join him for coffee. Her excuse—he'd approached her while in a vulnerable state. She rolled her eyes. Considering all her negative associations with men, she needed to be more wary of her choices.

Traveling the forty miles to Tremaine headquarters in Gig Harbor gave Jo enough time to ponder over her discoveries at the house and to confirm she'd made the right decision about Max. As the minutes rushed by, she was proud of herself for quelling the old gnawing at her self-worth.

She parked in Homestead Office Plaza's lot and locked her SUV. Hugging her briefcase close, she approached the wide, marble steps. A cross-country bike ride might not be on everyone's to-do list, but the activity went a long way to maintain Jo's sanity. No one in her bike club criticized her choice of clothes, her hair, her height. But all of the positives derived from the recent week-long trip on Washington State's Olympic Peninsula dissolved when she faced the building. Other than the email from Dad last night, she'd had no contact with anyone from the office during her vacation, and now she doubted she was ready to face daily doses of Mother's criticism and Serena's animosity.

Speaking of… Serena Kensington, her co-worker, descended the steps. Jo couldn't avoid her and forced a smile. "Good morning."

"Hi." She raised her thin, penciled eyebrows as she gave Jo the once-over. "Hmm. Nearly noon. Being the boss's daughter has its perks." Musky notes of her expensive perfume wafted around Jo.

She knew Serena goaded her, but she couldn't help reacting. "I've been checking on a rental property."

"Sure." Jingling her car keys, the diminutive blonde stepped backward. "By the way, I met a friend of yours in Seattle last week. He gave me something for you. I left it at reception." A quick smirk marred her flawless features for a second. "A lot has happened while you were gone. Your folks and I had a long chat about you. I just love your mother. She's such a stickler for propriety. I wouldn't be surprised if you're… Never mind. Gotta go." She waved over her shoulder and sauntered to her car.

Although they'd been college roommates years ago,

ever since Jo joined her parents' real estate company, Serena had become waspish, even hostile. To make matters worse, whenever in Serena's presence, Jo always felt like an awkward giant.

There was nothing she could do about her stature. She hurried into the building and took her place in one of the lines of customers at the coffee shop. Fortified by the nutty aroma, she focused on the baseball cap of the man in front of her and shoved the image of Serena from her mind. Jo needed nothing else to ruin her day. But what was the topic of Serena's conversation with her parents? The tension in Jo's neck multiplied. Maybe she'd read too much into the woman's veiled threat. At least Jo hadn't received a curt email from her mom.

A mother and young child joined the second line. The five- or six-year-old boy's wide-eyed stare traveled from Jo's sturdy leather boots slowly up to her face. In spite of her inner turmoil, she gave him a smile. Just then, his mother lowered her head and whispered in his ear. Jo had a good idea what she'd said.

Inches taller than most of the patrons, Jo drew back her shoulders and lifted her chin. Long ago she ceased being annoyed or embarrassed by gawking strangers. She'd heard all the tall remarks. What's the weather like up there? You must have played basketball in college, right? She towered over her girlfriends—many were a full head shorter—and she and her and were the same height.

Once Jo received her order, she gave the child a

little wave. He had no way of knowing how his awe-filled expression had lifted her spirits.

She crossed the marble foyer to the double doors of Tremaine Realty and gripped the cold metal handle. Anxiety knots invaded her stomach. All the confidence she'd mustered in line evaporated. Had Serena carried out her threat to divulge Jo's secret while she'd been on vacation? She squeezed her eyes tight. Now would be a good time to say a prayer—but she hadn't prayed in years.

Regrets over foolish decisions in her past darkened her mood even further. Abysmal choice in boyfriends. Trust in a business partner who betrayed her. Her breath whooshed out in a mammoth sigh. But she had a job. The salary helped pay off her debts and funded her passion of cross-country bicycling.

Loud voices from the coffee shop behind her beckoned Jo to the present. She had to face her parents. If Serena had not ratted on her, then she wouldn't let them into her dark past. Not yet. After all, she'd kept the secret for eight years. Why lower her mother's opinion of her even further?

She took a deep breath and pushed open the door into the lobby.

Lucia Ross, the dainty, raven-haired receptionist glanced up. "Welcome back. I'm so glad to see you."

Nothing strained in her greeting. Jo returned Lucia's grin. "Hi, Luce. I like your new glasses. Any messages?"

"Thanks. They're on your desk. Where'd you go this time?"

Jo ran a hand through her short curls. "We did the Olympic Discovery Trail. Started in Port Townsend, rode west along the Strait and ended in La Push on the Pacific Ocean coast. About two hundred miles, including several side trips. Best ride in ages. I'll tell you all about it during your lunch break."

"Check with your folks because I don't think you'll be here long. Oh, I almost forgot. Serena left this for you." Lucia handed her a small plastic bag, then adjusted the slim microphone at her mouth and answered an incoming call.

Certain the bag contained nothing of importance, except maybe another jibe from Serena, Jo shoved it into the side pouch of her briefcase. Not eager to find out what she'd be doing later, she hurried down the wide hall, hoping to reach her office without encountering her parents. But behind her came Mother's distinctive quick clipping heels. Jo turned.

Anita Tremaine opened her arms wide. "Joanna, darling. Come give me a hug."

A friendly greeting. Safe for now. Serena hadn't blabbed.

Jo cocked her head as she studied at her mother. How did she do it? Stylish mauve linen suit. Immaculate platinum chignon. Always photo-shoot ready.

"Hello, Mother." Jo bent to hug her and received a

peck on the cheek.

Anita slid one arm around Jo's waist and clicked her tongue. "What have you done to your hair?" Pointing, she frowned. "It's so frizzy and…red."

"Blame Daddy for that."

"Let me make an appointment for you with Antoine. He'll—"

"Mother, please don't. Nothing will help in this humidity. I'll use hairspray."

"At least you covered your freckles with foundation."

To distract her mother, Jo asked, "Where's Dad?"

Twisting her diamond tennis bracelet, Anita followed Jo into her office. "He has big news. I'll tell him you're here. But before you go out again, please do something with your hair." Her focus dropped to the floor. "Why do you insist on wearing those awful boots? There's nothing feminine about them. And another pair of brown slacks. Don't you own anything else?"

Jo sank into her leather chair and stowed her purse in the bottom drawer of her desk and set the briefcase against the wall. "Mother…"

With a shrug, Anita backed out of the large space. "I know, I know." At the door she stopped and patted her chignon. "Before Daddy comes, tell me about Max. Did anything significant happen between you?"

Willing nonchalance into her voice, Jo folded her arms. "Yes, he proposed, but—"

"Oh, darling, I'm so happy. You know I want more grandchildren." Anita rushed back, but halted when Jo stood. "But what?"

Crossed arms guarding her heart, Jo chose her words carefully. Describing another failed relationship hurt more than she cared to admit. "He wants me to quit my job and—"

"Then quit." Anita's pursed lips and head tilt communicated more than her words.

"And he wants me to quit the bike club."

"Oh, that." Anita dismissed the club with a flick of her hand. "It would be a blessing to us all if you gave up that nonsense."

"I enjoy the activities, and I have friends in the club."

"You can make other friends. What did you say to Max?"

Unseen hands squeezed Jo's throat. She swallowed against the pressure. "I told him no." No to quitting her job and the club, no to marriage, and no to his domineering ways. Never again would a man make her do something against her will.

"Let *me* talk to Max Hatfield." Anita drummed manicured pink nails on the glass-topped desk. "I'll tell him to ask again. After all, beg—"

"Anita, dear. Leave our Jo-Jo be." Thomas Tremaine entered the office and beamed at Jo. His balding head gleamed through thin, gray-streaked auburn hair.

Jo bolted into his out-stretched arms. He always seemed to arrive at the perfect time. Her hero. "Hello, Dad."

"Good to see you, punkin." He planted a kiss on her forehead. "I heard what you told Mother, and all I can say is good riddance. There's someone better than Max for you out there."

Jo returned to her desk and picked up the printed list of phone messages. "Mother says you have news, too." She plopped on the edge of her chair and read the first message from Scott Napier. The brief words didn't make sense. She set it aside and straightened pens in a holder. Unwrapped a square of her favorite dark chocolate and popped it into her mouth. Anything to appear happy and rational.

"Yes, indeed." Thomas sat at the round conference table. "Are you going to join us, honey?"

Anita shook her head and smoothed her skirt over her slim hips. "Joanna, did you visit Nelda's house?"

"Yes. It's a mess." Jo would rather not describe what she'd found with Mother in attendance. She would dissolve into hysterics, and no one would get any work done. "Why did you agree to take on the project?"

"Nelda's a school chum. When she called from Denver and disclosed the last renters left the house in a disgusting state, I told her as a special favor, we'd take care of it. Arrange for repairs, painting, yard work. Whatever it needs to get it ready to sell. No limit on financial outlay." Anita raised her perfectly arched eyebrows. "Nelda should have hired our property management staff. But that's another story."

"The house is in a beautiful setting."

"It is. I know you'll do a good job." Anita fingered her pearl necklace. "I'm meeting a client in ten minutes. Be sure to give Joanna all the news, dear. See you later." She gave Thomas a pat on the arm and closed the door behind her.

Thomas beamed. "I conducted interviews several weeks ago. Since business is picking up in Port Townsend, we added a seasoned agent there and hired a new guy to head the Silverdale office. Neither Wesley nor Ethan wanted that responsibility."

How will new employees in these branch offices affect me? Grimacing at her thought and the list of messages, Jo sipped her coffee. "Dad, is this new guy another one of your pet veteran projects?" Thomas had served twenty years in the US Marine Corps and hired veterans whenever he could—qualified or not.

Thomas slumped, his paunch almost touching the table. "Now, Jo. You know I don't like you referring to my guys like that. But, yes, Flynn McCaul in the Silverdale office is a former Marine."

"What are his qualifications?" Jo stared at the message list again. "Can he spell escrow?" She instantly regretted throwing out that insult, but with her dad as the exception, she was in no frame of mind to be generous to the male species. Jo glanced up. A deep frown covered her father's forehead. Her words had hurt him. "I'm sorry, Dad, but the last man you hired couldn't even use a computer."

His chuckle and quick change of demeanor surprised her. "This guy's different. He's worked in real estate for a couple of years and is a techno-whiz. In fact, he's streamlined our marketing ability and updated our search programs and data files. With so many options available to buyers or sellers, we have to be more competitive and creative. Flynn will provide training to all agents tomorrow at ten o'clock."

Errol Flynn, techno-wiz to the rescue! Jo smothered a smile. "All agents?"

"Uh-huh. Flynn and I finalized the details last Friday."

"Why didn't you add that to your email last night?"

"He wasn't sure if he'd conduct the workshop tomorrow or next week."

Jo drained her cup and threw it in the trash. "I see."

Eyeing the wall clock, Thomas pushed back from the table. "Thanks for taking on Nelda's property."

"I didn't want to upset Mother, but I won't be able to return there for a while." She described her unusual morning.

"That's got to be a first. Are you all right?"

"Yeah. Of course, the deputy wouldn't tell me how the blood ended up on Rosie's scarf. That reminds me. I need to send her the tenant's details."

"I emailed you their rental agreement from the other company."

Jo opened her laptop. "I'll take care of that right away."

"There's another message from me. We have prospective clients who might hire our services. Garland and Velma Adair just purchased a second home and want to rent it out. Can you squeeze in a meeting today?"

"Of course. Before I organize the work projects on Nelda's house, do I need to confer with Flynn?"

"I almost forgot. Flynn has another responsibility that will affect you."

More changes? "What's that?"

"In conjunction with heading the Silverdale office, he'll coordinate all the contractors and supervise their work. We were having a hard time finding reliable people who'd do small jobs for us. Flynn also works parttime for his brother-in-law's construction company."

Jo held back a retort, but the words congealed in her mind. *Computer and construction genius. His name should be Jack. Jack of all... Stop.*

She huffed out a sigh.

"One more thing, punkin." Thomas stood and adjusted his striped navy tie. "Don't let your mother's obsession with marrying you off bother you. When the right man comes along, you'll know it. As far as I'm concerned, you never have to marry. I just want you to be happy."

Blinking back tears, Jo sprang from her chair to

accept his embrace. "You're right, Dad, but I get so tired of being compared to Kendall." She yanked a tissue out of a box on her desk and swiped at her eyes.

"Your sister is a remarkable woman, but so are you. I'm proud of you both." Thomas squeezed Jo's arm. "Don't be too hard on Flynn. Give him a chance, okay?"

She nodded, crumpled the tissue, and returned to her desk. The troubling message glared at her. "Wait, Dad. I need to ask you a question." She picked up the list and held it out to him. "Look at the first message. What do you know about the Napier deal?"

Thomas squinted. "Ah, yes. Scott and Donna closed on the Bainbridge Island property Friday."

"But they agreed to wait until I returned."

"Really? That's not what I heard." Thomas reached his right hand across and tugged on his left earlobe, a habitual gesture when agitated. "You'd best check with Serena. She handled everything. With your blessing, or so she said."

Sinking into the chair, Jo rubbed her stomach. She should have purchased a sandwich along with her coffee.

"I take it you didn't give Serena the go-ahead?"

A pool of quicksand in Jo's throat seemed to swallow her words. She shook her head and clamped her mouth shut, sure if she spoke, her father would blush at her choice of words.

Thomas leaned against the door frame. "She won't

be attending the training in Silverdale. You'll have to straighten it out with her later. Sorry, punkin."

His words took a second to penetrate, then Jo glared at him. "Why not? I thought you said all agents had to attend."

"Serena worked with Flynn developing protocols. She—"

"I was only gone two weeks. This upgrade must have been in the works long before I left."

Thomas's cheeks took on a rosy tint. "Now, Jo-Jo, don't get upset. I didn't involve you because I know your heart's not in this job. Don't get me wrong— you're a great agent, but one of these days when your finances are in better shape, you'll leave us to start your own company. But this time it will be a success."

Although true, Dad's words still stung. Yeah, Jo gave her best, but in her soul she knew, and apparently so did he, the real estate business was just a stepping stone.

He cleared his throat. "While we're discussing your future, thank you for agreeing to transfer so Wesley can work here in Gig Harbor."

"He certainly made the long commute to Silverdale for years and he's talked about the move before. Why now?"

"There's an opening at the Bradfield Group Home in Tacoma for their son, and Wesley wants to work closer to home, especially now his wife's health is deteriorating."

Jo had often talked with Wesley about Noah, and she had met him numerous times at company picnics. The young adult had Williams Syndrome, and naturally his parents were concerned about his future. "Does Err…I mean does the new guy know?"

"Flynn and I discussed the possibility."

"Good. I'll check with Wesley, and we'll make the trade as soon as he's ready."

Thomas approached the desk, bent and kissed her forehead again "Thanks, my dear child. For all your bravado, you have a kind heart."

A trickle of guilt washed over Jo. Sure, she agreed to the transfer for Wesley's sake, but she'd also benefit. Closer to her apartment in Bremerton, less contact with Serena, and she'd be away from Mother's fault-finding eyes.

Chapter 4

Briefcase bulging with personal folders she wanted to transfer to her new location clutched under her arm, and her bowl of chocolates secure in her purse, Jo closed her office door. Walking down the hall, she revisited the discussion about Serena. She'd poached Jo's clients and earned a whopping commission on a multimillion-dollar mansion. That money could have whittled down Jo's debt and kept her in specialized bike accessories for years. She frowned and plotted ways to get even. Then wiped the negative thoughts away. Revenge was not her style.

As Jo entered the reception area, Lucia gestured from the counter. "Can you take over for a minute? I need a restroom break and my replacement is late."

"Sure." Jo set her things behind the curved desk, then wandered to the sleek metal and glass coffee table beside two comfortable armchairs and straightened brochures and magazines. Her phone rang and she slipped it out of her pocket.

"Hey, Kendy."

"Afternoon, sis. Mother called and told me about Max. I'm so sorry. Want to come over for dinner tonight and bad-mouth him?"

Jo giggled. Her sister always knew how to pull her out of a funk. "Love to. I'll bring the dessert. How are the kids?"

"Pretty good. They're excited to hear about your trip."

"I'll download pictures for them."

They visited a minute longer then Jo hung up and sat at Lucia's desk, doodling on a notepad while thinking of her sister. Twenty-nine-year-old Kendall—two years her senior—seemed to have the perfect life. Along with her successful husband and two adorable kids, she lived in a spacious home in Tacoma. Despite having a degree in marketing, she homeschooled Kasi aged seven and Blake aged five. Her lush brunette locks complemented her porcelain complexion, her dark eyes were fringed with long lashes. And no one criticized Kendy's five-foot-seven height.

A call on the business phone interrupted Jo's musing. She answered the client's question, swiveled, and crossed her booted ankles on the credenza. Kendy had always been a caring big sister, and Jo did not envy her—except for maybe her lack of inches.

After answering another call, Jo stared at her boots. Her mother never failed to criticize them. Jo shrugged. Maybe that's why she wore them almost every day. Besides, her favorite boots were comfortable, and who knew where the next client might want to go? Tremaine Realty specialized in offering country living at its best, prime waterfront properties. Sometimes showing a property involved walking through deposits left by country living animals. Not to mention the mud.

Which reminded Jo of her recent foray into Nelda's barn and her confusion when she'd opened the rental agreement the original property management company provided. No mention of Wade or Rosie. Charles Freeman signed the documents. Jo had forwarded the details to Deputy Frances Gordon. Maybe she could unravel the mystery. And then Jo could either ditch the shoebox of little toys or hand it over to Mr. Freeman. For now, she'd leave it in her SUV.

A bald man entered from the lobby and headed straight for Jo. Lean and tall, dressed in a dark blue suit, his attitude exuded determination.

Jo hastily set her feet on the floor and stood. "Welcome to Tremaine Realty, sir. How may I help you?"

His smile displayed white teeth with a gold cap sparkling on one molar. "Good afternoon, Miss." He hesitated and glanced at the photograph-lined waiting area. "I have a strange request. I'm looking for a realtor, but not because I want to purchase property. I need to find a man."

Jo squelched a giggle. "I assume you don't know his name?"

"Correct. By the way, I'm Lewis Pierce. I'm

looking for a man who dated my sister. I saw him once from a distance, so I only have a general description. But I was given your company's name as a possibility."

Jo pointed to the row of color photographs. "Check out our agents. These people work here and in our surrounding branch offices." She glanced at her portrait. Shoulder-length auburn waves surrounded her face. What a bother that hairstyle had been to maintain. She patted her short curls and smiled. Mother was not a fan of the change.

Mr. Pierce scanned pictures of the men and shook his head. "These are the same people on your website, and I don't see him. He's in his mid-thirties, well built. Thank you anyway."

"Sorry."

Lucia hummed as she approached the desk.

"Oh, wait Mr. Pierce. We have a couple of new-hires whose pictures are not displayed yet." Jo turned to the receptionist. "Luce, do you have photographs of the new agents?"

"I do." Lucia rummaged through papers on the desk. "Somewhere."

"Please let Mr. Pierce see them. I have to leave, sir. Hope you find your man. Good-bye." She grabbed her belongings and stepped to the door. An idea shot into her mind. The Adairs agreed to meet her at their new property in Brownsville which was close to Silverdale. She could stop at the office and meet Errol Flynn. And chat with Wesley.

Her reflection in the glass door glared at her. A frizzy auburn mess crowned her head. Jo entered the restroom to *do something* with her hair. Mother would be pleased. She dampened the curls, ran her fingers through and spritzed puffs of hairspray, then turned her head side to side. Her hair did look more controlled, but other than a complete head shave, nothing would keep those curls in line. She straightened the lapels of her saffron yellow shirt. At least her mother hadn't also criticized the color. Jo had learned in her late teens to make the most of her red hair and chose clothes that emphasized the unusual shade. Go bold and receive compliments or get noticed for your height, had become her mantra.

With a heavy sigh, she continued to the exit doors. On the steps outside she spied Lewis Pierce, talking animatedly on his cell phone. She slowed near a large column to eavesdrop.

He sounded excited. "Yes, I located him. He has an office in Silverdale. He'd better be ready to tell me about Geena. We haven't found her yet."

Hmm. Was Errol Flynn McCaul in trouble? Jo covertly used her cellphone to take a photo of Lewis. Now she had a legitimate reason for visiting Flynn. However, on her way north out of Gig Harbor, she encountered backed up traffic and changed her mind. A detour to see the man wouldn't have taken long, but she wanted to grab a bite to eat before her meeting. Besides, she'd be in the Silverdale office the next day.

The scenic thirty-five-mile drive helped set her mind in a positive direction. Not having to face Serena for at least two days added to her optimism. Jo located a restaurant and downed a bowl of clam chowder. With time to spare, she parked along the street close to the Adair's new home and opened her window. Savory aromas of grilling meat from a house close by wafted into her vehicle. Even although she'd had lunch, her mouth watered. She extracted a contract and brochure describing what Tremaine Property Management offered from her briefcase.

While flipping through the colorful leaflet, her phone rang. Scott Napier. "Hi, Scott." Recalling Serena's interference, resentment roiled in Jo's gut.

"I just spoke with your dad, Jo. I'm so sorry about what happened. We were all set to wait for your return, but, well, we—"

"I said I'd be back in two weeks." Clenching her teeth, Jo struggled to remain civil.

"I know, but we were in the office last week and bumped into Serena. She asked about our housing situation and mentioned that you might not be returning to the company."

"Obviously, that's not true."

"I know that now, and I, we, are so sorry." Scott cleared his throat. "I should have talked with Thomas, but Serena was very convincing."

Jo had nothing to add.

"Other than to apologize, the reason I'm calling is

to tell you we have friends who also want to relocate to Bainbridge. I've given them your contact details. So, please, if you hear from Tony and Helen Underwood, give them your best. As you did for us, until I blew it."

"Thank you for the referral. I look forward to working with them." Jo ended the call before her voice cracked. Serena was vindictive and mean.

And she'd met a friend of Jo's in Seattle. She located Serena's plastic bag in the side pouch of her briefcase and peeked inside. It contained a square, ecru envelope which she removed, holding it between thumb and forefinger as if it contained rat poison. She stared at the scrawled handwriting. The curvy *J* jolted her memory.

Fingers trembling, Jo ripped into the envelope. Abstract designs in purple and blue swarmed over the front of the card. She opened it. Her vision blurred and she blinked.

> *Jo, I'm so glad Serena contacted me. She said you want to talk. Great. I'm sorry for the hurt I caused you, but I'm divorced now. After all these years, I still care for you and have forgiven you. Call me, please. I have the same phone number.*
> *Phil Baldwin.*

The words sliced through her heart.

Teeth clenched, Jo slammed her fist into her thigh

over and over. Talk to him? Never. Jagged memories stabbed her brain like an ice pick chipping away the frozen surface—the hurt and embarrassment of discovering during her wedding service that her fiancé was already married. She could still hear the minister's voice. "Does anyone know of any just reason why this couple…" He didn't even complete his question before a woman stood up at the back of the church and yelled, "Stop. He's still married to me!"

Jo shook her head to dislodge the image and groaned. As if that wasn't enough, two months later she'd had a miscarriage with complications, followed by deep depression and thoughts of suicide. Since she'd been diagnosed with emotional or dissociative amnesia about that time, the random details she recalled were enough to send her close to the edge of reason.

Tears formed but she refused to let them fall. She swiped them away and focused on the bank of gray clouds marching toward the sun. Muggy heat of the July day and the reminder of the man who almost destroyed her life surrounded her in a suffocating mantle. She'd been so flattered by the attention of such a sophisticated, older man that she allowed him to compromise her values which resulted in the pregnancy.

Unable to stop herself, Jo reread the words. *Forgive her?* The nerve of the man. Forgive her for punching him in the face, running out of the building and scratching his fancy convertible with her…his diamond ring? What jilted bride wouldn't have done the same? Or worse?

Jo took a deep breath, thumping her chest as if to revive her heart beat. She ripped the card in two, then shredded it into tiny pieces and tossed the confetti over her shoulder. Blood thundered in her brain like an approaching stampede. She wrapped her arms tightly around her body and lowered her head. She spied a piece of Phil's card on her thigh. A new wave of shame and guilt ripped a chasm in her chest. Struggling to breathe, she picked up the scrap and tossed it aside. Surely eight years was enough time to forget, but every detail of that day, that year, was etched anew onto her heart.

Eyes closed, she sat for minutes. Or hours. She was numb and filled with the old self-loathing that had engulfed her after her miscarriage. Any confidence she'd developed over the last several years evaporated. She despised her ungainly, awkward body that couldn't even keep a baby alive. Why was she trying to live a normal life?

A slow-moving vehicle drove past her and entered the property. Jo wanted to run away, hide, divorce herself from society. How could she put on a professional façade and meet new clients? But she had a job to do. She would not disappoint her parents. For the second time that day, she checked her reflection. Same result. Blotchy skin and red nose. She scrambled in her purse for a tissue and dabbed at her eyes.

Seasonal allergies could account for her appearance. The Adairs needn't know she had none.

She drove to the house, removed the excess files from her briefcase, and carried the slimmed-down version to the front door. Her phone set on vibrate buzzed in her pocket, indicating a text. She peeked at the screen. Serena. Against all common sense, Jo opened the message.

Phil's eager to meet. I gave him your address, phone number, and email.

Ready to confront Serena even if she had to drive all over the Kitsap Peninsula, Jo turned to rush away, but Velma Adair opened the door.

"You must be Joanna Tremaine. Please, come in."

Chapter 5

Another monkey-suit day. Flynn shoved his arms into the navy sports jacket and scowled. He'd much prefer to wear jeans and a polo shirt, but he had to put on a show. The boss's daughter would grace their presence and he was anxious to impress her, especially since she'd be working in his office soon. He tugged on the lapels. Shoulders were a bit snug. Better ease up on the weightlifting or buy bigger clothes.

A step around the desk produced a pain that took his breath away. He paused to knead his left thigh. If he could sit through most of the presentation, he should be able to handle the discomfort. He'd overdone the walking yesterday and although intense dagger-sharp zaps down his leg reminded him frequently, he chose to leave his cane in his office.

In the large conference room, he set a stool in front of the podium that held his laptop. He clicked on the presentation folder and focused the image displayed on the large white screen. Seven chairs in place along one side of the oblong table, bottled water and soda cans in a tub of ice. All set.

A knock on the door.

Flynn turned too quickly. Sharp twinges shot through his left calf and foot. Grimacing, he greeted the office manager. "Hey, Brian. We're ready. Send the agents in when they arrive." He sank onto the stool and massaged his calf.

"Will do. The food delivery from Seafood, Etcetera is scheduled for twelve." Brian adjusted his colorful bowtie. "You okay?"

"Yeah." Flynn gave his calf one last squeeze. "But the nerve pain is severe this morning."

A hint of pity flickered in his gaze. "Do you need your cane?"

"No, thanks." Flynn had educated his coworkers about his injuries and physical limitations but hated when they treated him like an invalid. They meant well, but he wanted nothing more than to be regarded as a normal, healthy human being.

The phone rang. Brian returned to the reception desk.

Flynn moved the lectern over a fraction then joined Brian in reception and sank onto the low leather couch. A barrage of phone calls bombarded the young man. For several minutes, he answered questions or forwarded calls to Ethan or Wesley, the other Silverdale agents.

Another call and he looked at Flynn. "This one's for you."

Without his cane, Flynn struggled to stand. "I'll

take it in my office." He settled at his desk and picked up the receiver. "Flynn McCaul speaking. How may I help you?"

"Flynn McCaul, I've had a hard time finding you."

He pulled the receiver away from his ear and stared at the object as if it crawled with germs. "Who is this?"

"We've never met." The man's words held a hint of menace. "My name is Lewis Pierce, Geena's brother."

The name ripped a hole in Flynn's heart. He swallowed and straightened in his chair. "How…what do you want?"

Silence jammed the line as if it were interference.

"Lewis, are you still there?"

"Yeah, and I'll soon be in your face." He paused a moment then spewed out the next words. "Where. Is. My. Sister?"

Sweat beaded along Flynn's hairline. "Wait, I never knew she had a brother."

"You do now. Where is she?"

"I don't know. That's the truth."

"You think I'll take your word for it? You were the last person to see her alive."

He couldn't remember much about his drug induced days in the hospital after the explosion except for Geena's face swimming in and out of focus through the haze. Until she backed out of his hospital room, saying, "I can't deal with all this talk of you losing a leg."

Flynn's heart beat surged. "She left in July, four years ago. I haven't seen her since." Voices drifted through his open door. The agents had arrived. "I must go. Can we discuss this later?"

"I'll call you again. Watch your back." Lewis hung up before Flynn could respond.

He stood, manufacturing a smile as he left his office. Lewis's threat would have to wait.

Brian introduced the guests he ushered into the conference room. Flynn noted characteristics to help him remember each person. He welcomed lanky and gaunt Tanner Jones whose dark brown suit coordinated with his skin tone, Alec Zinsmeyer, almost as round as he was tall, and Camille Burns wearing a long multi-colored, flowing dress and a bright orange band which held her gray hair off her face. All from Port Townsend.

A few minutes later, another car parked outside, and a man climbed out. He removed the tan fedora from his bald head, tweaked his dark mustache, and came inside where he hugged Brian. "Good to see you, young man. Congratulations. When's the baby due?"

"Next month." He beamed. "Flynn, this is Hal Wakelin from Gig Harbor."

The men shook hands and Hal entered the conference room to a barrage of greetings. Flynn followed and made his way to the front. Ethan and Wesley were already seated.

At ten o'clock, Flynn handed out copies of abbreviated notes. "Welcome, everyone. You can add details to the notes as we go through the presentation. Water and soda are in the tub on the side table and lunch will be delivered later."

He perched on his stool and noted the empty chair. Perhaps the boss's daughter couldn't tell time. "I assume Joanne didn't ride with you, Hal?"

"No. Maybe she's with Serena."

"Serena's not coming. She helped me with the presentation." The mere mention of her name and he began to heat up.

He fanned his face with his notes and turned to the screen. The words in his introduction wavered across the blue background. What was happening? Was he losing control? A boulder lodged in his throat. He needed a drink and fresh air.

Slipping off the stool, he headed to the door. "I'll be right back, folks." He grabbed a bottle of water and screwed off the cap.

In the reception area he loosened his tie and glugged down half the bottle. Not a panic attack, surely? But when he closed his eyes, he was back in the demolished cabin, his parents moaning, his siblings screaming. And pain slicing through his leg. *No, no. Not again.* Drawing in a deep breath, he opened his eyes and moved to the window. Distraction. Focus on inane objects. The vehicles out front. Two black sedans. A motorbike. Green pickup. Blue delivery van.

After going through the vehicles twice, the churning in his gut settled. He straightened his tie, preparing to face the agents when a neon-yellow SUV with a bike rack on the rear stopped at the corner. Probably

Joanna's vehicle. Serena told him she drove an ugly yellow vehicle.

Flynn had no desire to be caught waiting for the boss's daughter. He turned too quickly. Off balance, he stumbled over the umbrella stand and landed on his rump. He sucked in air as pain rammed through his leg. The rigid brace designed to help him walk without tripping had twisted in his shoe, adding to his discomfort.

Rolling up his left trouser, he removed the shoe. "Doggone it." He corrected the brace but couldn't linger. Joanna might discover him on the floor. He pulled himself upright and hopped into his office as the nerves in his foot and calf burned as if a thousand fire ants nipped his flesh.

Chapter 6

Although she'd had a productive afternoon following her meltdown the previous day, Jo still had a lingering headache, and being late only added to her anxiety. She'd dropped the shoebox and the toys had scattered all over her bedroom where she'd left them, and then she spilled creamer on her blouse and slacks. She changed into charcoal twill pants and an emerald-green silk top. A little fancy, but she had no time to be choosy. The short drive from her apartment in Bremerton to the office in Silverdale on Bucklin Hill Road took all of ten minutes, and as she neared her destination, her thoughts veered to Flynn. Dad's vague description of his latest protégée concerned her. Flynn had imitations when it came to showing properties. Why? Was the guy shortsighted? In a wheelchair?

Jo turned into the parking lot and slammed on the brakes. A silver pickup with a handicap license plate occupied the reserved spot in front of the office. The mechanism for raising and lowering a wheelchair fixed in the bed of the truck pointed an accusing arm at her.

Swallowing her shame, she parked, and hurried up the steps. Dad omitted to tell her the guy was physically disabled.

On entering the deserted reception area, she noticed Brian in the office to her left conversing with a seated man. *It's Flynn. In a wheelchair.* Heat rose up her neck as she clutched the silk fabric over her heart. Apology ready, she took a feeble step forward. But how could she apologize for her thoughts?

Brian approached her. "Jo. So good to see you again. Come on in. We're meeting in the conference room." He headed down the hall. "Can I get you a soda?"

She shook her head but kept her attention on Flynn. In a navy suit jacket, his shoulders were almost as wide as the desk. His mouth formed something halfway between a smile and a smirk. She was late, but he didn't have to rub it in.

"Sorry I'm late, Mr. McCaul."

He leaned to the left and winced. The overhead light shone on his wavy blondish hair. "That's all right, Miss Tremaine. You haven't missed anything."

"Please, call me Jo."

"Not Joanna?" He pushed away from the desk.

Here it comes. He'll wheel his chair out from behind the desk, and arrows of guilt will point at me. With eyes glued to his arms, she said, "Only Mother calls me Joanna."

Flynn stood and stepped around the desk.

Jo almost choked. He could walk. The pickup wasn't his. Relief cascaded over her in a cool shower. He walked stiffly toward her and she extended her hand. "Welcome to Tremaine Realty."

Her hand almost disappeared in his calloused paw, and she had to raise her head a fraction to look into his gray eyes.

"Pleased to meet you, Jo." His tone held a note of something, maybe derision. It wasn't the first time an employee had shown her disdain for being a Tremaine.

She turned to hide the expression she feared displayed vestiges of her guilt and joined the other agents in the conference room.

Flynn strode to the front in spite of a slight limp. After dimming the lights, he perched on a stool and began his presentation. Animated and personable, he held the audience's attention with his expert knowledge and ready smile which he'd withheld from Jo at their initial meeting.

As he talked, Jo scribbled notes while studying him from her dim corner. He had former-Marine stamped all over. Pulled back shoulders, the take-charge attitude. He wore authority like a well-fitting uniform.

At the conclusion of his presentation, Jo had to admit the changes Flynn introduced would streamline their search capabilities and allow agents to customize their databases. For once, Dad's hiring choice panned out.

Brian brought in boxed lunches—a selection of

lobster rolls, salmon salad, and roasted vegetable sandwiches. The agents made their choices while the office manager rearranged chairs around the table.

Seated at one end, Jo welcomed Wesley to join her. They had much to discuss. She opened her box and the subtle aroma of grilled salmon wafted out. "Have you told anyone else of your upcoming move?" After pouring raspberry vinaigrette over the salad, she glanced at him. Middle-aged and scrawny, he had the sweetest temperament and doted on his wife and five adult children.

With a mouth full of lobster, he shook his head.

Across the table, Camille's mention of Serena spiked the little hairs on the back of Jo's neck. "When do you want to transfer?" The sooner the better. Even thinking about facing that woman daily made her blood curdle. Besides avoiding Mother's questions about Max and marriage, maybe, with a little distance, Jo would be able to tell her parents about Phil and the baby.

Wesley arched his bushy, brown, caterpillar eyebrows. "I have no open leads, and to tell the truth, I've been so worried about Iris's health and Noah's future, I've neglected my job. I'm so glad Flynn is here now. And you will make a great addition to the team. I'm ready to make the change as soon as you are."

"Good. Let's discuss the timeframe with Flynn."

"Thanks. You'll enjoy working with Ethan and Brian."

Hmm. He said nothing about Flynn.

Wesley's phone jingled. He checked the screen. "It's Iris. I'll take the call in the foyer." Worry lines creasing his face, he left the room, phone to his ear.

Spanish words flew back and forth at the other end of the table. Flynn talking to Alec and Tanner. Great. The man, now with his jacket discarded and shirtsleeves rolled up above his elbows, was not only a computer whiz, but was also bilingual. What other talents did he possess? Jo clenched her fist, her nails biting into her palm. She had to stop this sarcasm. She hardly knew the guy and planned to work with him in the near future.

The other agents left soon after the meal, but Jo lingered so she could tell Flynn about Lewis Pierce and her swap with Wesley, who'd not returned yet. She helped Brian clean up the conference room and waited for an opportunity to approach Flynn. When he carried his laptop to his office, she followed.

"Mr. McCaul, the changes you developed will greatly benefit this company. Thank you. Do you have a minute to discuss another issue?"

He loosened his tie and sank into his chair, a bland expression on his face. "Please, call me Flynn."

Jo sat in one of the office chairs and crossed her legs. The smile he'd given her colleagues never made an appearance. Had he only agreed to her transfer to please Dad? "First of all, a man named Lewis Pierce came to our office yesterday looking for you."

A frown created a *V* between his brows. "He called

me." Flynn rocked back and forth in his chair, then leaned forward and focused his steel gray eyes on her. "Did he tell you what he wanted?"

Hiking one shoulder, Jo plucked at a fold in her pants. "He said you dated his sister." She didn't want to divulge the information she'd overheard until she had a better idea of the circumstances.

"Is that all?" Flynn yanked off his tie.

Fascinated by the chameleon like emotions flashing across Flynn's face, she nodded. "Where is his sister?"

A scowl strong enough to wither foliage beamed at her. "I don't know." He opened his laptop and punched a key. "Will there be anything else, Jo? I have a lot of work to do."

So much for prying. She focused on the muscle pulsing along his square jaw line. He really wanted her out of there, but she had to finalize the transfer date. She drew in a deep breath to gather courage and spied a Bible on his desk. He must be pretty secure in his faith to display it so openly.

She exhaled. "There is one other item. Dad informed you about Wesley and I trading places. We'd like to make the change as soon as possible."

Flynn's head jerked up.

In an attempt to soften her words, Jo shrugged. "Neither of us has any reason to prolong the switch."

Rocking back in the chair, Flynn clasped his hands over his flat abs and raised his eyebrows. "I guess if Thomas approves a quick transfer then I can't object."

Can't object? But he would if he could? "Has Wesley discussed why he wants to move? If not, you should ask him." Jo's growing positive opinion of Flynn took a nosedive.

"I'll miss him." Flynn returned to his computer and tapped the keys. "I'll wait to hear from Wesley. Where is he, by the way?" He glanced up but didn't stop typing. "I'm sure you and I will get along…fine."

Jo picked up her purse and stood. She couldn't tell if his curt reaction was due to the mention of Lewis Pierce, or to her desire to transfer. Assuming the latter, she stormed out of the office and waved to Brian occupied in an intense phone conversation at the reception counter.

Once in her vehicle, she took stock of her reaction to Flynn's statement. Could be his people skills needed work or he reserved them for clients and favored employees. Maybe he resented being stuck with the boss's daughter. In that case, she'd have to show the *former Marine* she knew the real estate business better than most.

Traffic on Highway 16 South slowed as it approached Gig Harbor, and Jo's stomach churned. Before leaving Silverdale, she'd called Lucia to check if Selena was in her office. Given an affirmative, Jo determined to confront the vindictive woman before packing up the rest of her personal items and the contractor files. Since she'd have to confer with Flynn about repairs to Nelda's house when given the okay, she might as well hit the ground running. That meeting would be easy compared to what she had planned for Serena.

Jo stormed across the foyer and stopped short in the reception area. Lucia had mounted photographs of the new-hires.

Alec Zinsmeyer, the new agent in the Port Townsend office, appeared as she recalled from their meeting that morning. Short, black curls surrounded his chubby face and his pleasant smile produced crinkles by the sides of his dark eyes. Flynn McCaul actually smiled in his headshot, too. Jo studied his face more closely. Although his smile bared perfect white teeth, his eyes remained cold and almost melancholy. Jo cocked her head. *Why so sad, Mr. McCaul?* Maybe she'd ask Dad more about him.

She turned toward the reception desk. "Luce, is my dad in?"

"Yes. I believe he's in the conference room." Lucia applied crimson lipstick and smacked her lips together. "How'd the training go?"

"Fine. Mr. McCaul sure knows his stuff. I'll be with Dad if anyone needs me. Oh, is Serena still here?" Jo headed to the hall and stopped.

"She's with a client. Do you want me to give her a message?"

Jo shook her head and hurried to the conference room before she lost her nerve. Dad sat at the head of the large, oval mahogany table with files spread out before him.

"Hey, Dad. Can I talk to you a minute?" Jo dumped her purse and briefcase on the table and sat next to him.

Thomas adjusted his glasses. "Of course, punkin. What's up? Hope it's got nothing to do with Flynn."

"Indirectly, it does. Are you sure he's okay with the transfer? He didn't seem too eager when I spoke to him."

"What are you two discussing in secret?" Anita entered the room and placed a hand on Thomas's shoulder but her gaze fixed on her daughter's face. "You're up to something."

"Have a seat, dear. Jo and Wesley are going to trade offices."

An impish smile tugged at the corners of her mouth. "Aha. I knew you'd like Flynn. He's good-looking, isn't he?"

Jo rested her elbows on the table. "Mother, it has nothing to do with Flynn. Didn't Dad tell you about Wesley's son?"

Anita's smile disappeared, but she kept her eyes on Jo. "Yes, but I didn't think you would agree to the move."

"Why not?" She didn't want an answer. "Wesley's long years of service deserve consideration, and I don't mind."

"In that case, I'm okay with the transfer. You'll do fine in Silverdale. Stop by the Hillside Bible Fellowship and say hello to the pastor, Orin Willoughby. He went to university with Daddy and me."

"Mother, I'm not moving to Silverdale."

"But you live close by. Just thought I'd mention the church. They meet in a rented hall. Flynn said he planned to attend."

"I assure you Flynn is onboard with the switch." Thomas leaned back and tugged on his earlobe. "Do you have any open contracts?"

Anger on a soft simmer stirred in Jo's gut. "The only one I had was the Napier's, but Serena handled it." Reminded of her next mission, she pushed back and grabbed her belongings. "Thanks, Mom and Dad. I appreciate all you do for me."

Striding down the hall, she chewed her lower lip. She did appreciate her folks. They'd bailed her out of a devastating financial loss in Seattle, but why couldn't Mother keep her nose out of Jo's religious affairs? Or lack of them.

Jo's steps slowed. A chink appeared in the amnesia shield around her past and she glimpsed a wispy memory concerning Mother. What was it? But it dissolved as quickly as a snowflake on a griddle pan. She shook her head and kept walking.

Outside Serena's office, Jo stopped. *Keep it civil. Keep it professional.*

She knocked.

A saccharin voice called, "Come in."

Jo opened the door and closed it immediately. What she had to say needed no audience. Rehearsed words scrambled in her brain. She blinked and inhaled. "This has got to stop, Serena. Stealing my clients is one thing, but contacting Phil was low—even for you."

Serena eyed Jo up and down. "Please sit. I get a crick in my neck looking up so far."

How had their relationship deteriorated so far? In college Serena was the one friend who never teased Jo about her height. She shook off the memories and concealed her fists in her pockets. Glaring down at the blonde, she fought to keep a sneer from forming. "You win this round. I'm transferring to Silverdale. You can even have my corner office, but leave my personal life alone."

A sneer stained Serena's refined features. "So, the big guy got to you?"

"What?"

"Flynn. You think you have a chance with him?"

Why did everyone assume she was after Flynn? "No. Not interested. I'm serious, Serena. Leave me alone."

"Or what? You gonna tell Mummy and Daddy on me?"

Momentarily lost for a reply, Jo opened the door. "No, I'm not a snitch."

Back in her office, breathing hard as if she'd run through the building, she drew her laptop from her briefcase and with trembling fingers, turned it on. After checking her calendar, she emailed Wesley and asked him if he could move the next day. She only had two clients who required follow-up meetings.

Forcing herself to relax, she stared out the window. At some point she'd have to tell her parents her secret. Then Serena would have no hold over her.

As Jo reviewed the notes she'd taken at the training session, her mother poked her head around the door. "Joanna, dear. I sense a little animosity between you and Serena. She's a real sweetheart. Why don't you try to patch up your differences? You were such close friends."

Blood on a slow boil, Jo clenched her jaw. She couldn't respond without screaming and just shook her head. For once, Mother took the hint and closed the door. Jo had no idea how long she sat dead-still while her anger cooled. Today would be her last day in the Gig Harbor office. Even if she had to work out of her car.

After the tense interactions she'd experienced, she needed a moral boost and called her club mates, Danny, Emma, and Vic to see if any of the team could meet for a meal and a chat. Danny agreed, and they arranged a time and place.

Drawn back to her computer by her alternating screensaver photos, Jo tapped a key, interested to see if Wesley had responded to her email yet.

But the only new message came from Phil Baldwin.

Chapter 7

At five-thirty on the dot, Flynn locked the office door and limped to his pickup. He glared at the hoist. Maybe it was time to have that thing removed. If he needed a wheelchair now, he could maneuver it himself. Not like when he'd first been discharged from rehab and the pain in his shoulder was so intense he couldn't even use his left arm. As if on command, he rolled his shoulder. Only a slight twinge—not enough to worry about.

He had one stop to make before driving to his condo on the outskirts of Silverdale—the small hall a local gymnastics club used several days a week. Balmy, briny air surrounded him as he climbed out of his truck. Much more tolerable than temperatures inland. During his first week in town, he'd inquired about using the gym space to hold self-defense classes in the late afternoons. To honor his mother, he'd provided the service in Spokane once he'd recovered from his injuries. Since he didn't charge for his services, he negotiated a nominal rental fee, and needed to sign the contract. Done. He'd advertise classes to begin the following week, Tuesday at six. More classes would be added if the need arose. After supper, he would create a flyer, print copies, and sometime tomorrow, ask to display them in grocery stores. While in town, he'd inform the sheriff's department, too. Maybe they could refer vulnerable women they met during their day-to-day encounters.

Satisfied with the deal and his plan, he drove home. On his way to the front door, a sleek black sedan drew up at the curb. Flynn didn't recognize the driver.

However, the man hailed him. "Flynn McCaul. Hold up. I need to talk to you."

The voice. It had to be Lewis Pierce.

Flynn leaned against the porch railing to relieve the pressure on his foot. "You're Geena's brother? How'd you know where I live?"

"Followed you." Lewis joined Flynn on the porch. "May I come in?"

Hot, tired, and in pain, Flynn had no energy to argue. The visitor had a scowl on his face, but otherwise didn't seem to pose a physical threat. "Sure."

Lewis followed Flynn into the living room.

"Do me a favor, please. Open the windows, back and front. The cross-breeze is the only air conditioning I need. I'll join you in a minute." Any other time, Flynn would not have left a guest—albeit an uninvited one—alone, but he had to remove his brace and thick socks.

Once in the bedroom, he shed his office garb, the *L*-

shaped brace, and his damp socks. He examined his foot. The brace had rubbed blisters on his heel and the strap holding the contraption in place had dug into his calf. No wonder it hurt. If the irritation and pain continued, he'd have to visit his prosthetist. Maybe his muscles had atrophied more, and he'd need a new custom brace. Compromised flesh was his new enemy.

Flynn donned denim shorts and a tank shirt. He usually didn't expose his withered leg or his scars to strangers, but Lewis had chosen the time of this meeting, and Flynn had no desire to protect his sensibilities. Using his cane, he hobbled to the kitchen. "Want something to drink?" he asked over the counter.

"A beer."

Grinning, Flynn opened the refrigerator. "Don't have any. How about iced tea or a soda?"

"So what I heard about you is true. A teetotaler."

"And proud of it. What will it be?"

"Soda."

Flynn grabbed two cans of Coke in one hand and made his way to the living room.

As soon as Lewis saw his leg, he stood, mouth agape. "I...didn't know. Sorry."

With a shrug, Flynn set the cans on the coffee table, sank into his recliner, and allowed the cane to clatter to the hardwood floor. He figured Lewis would ask about his injuries and steeled himself against repeating the events. Geena was part of his life back then, and he couldn't talk about her without reliving every part of it.

Flynn took a long swig of soda. Might as well get it over with. "What can I do for you?"

The man plopped on the edge of the sofa and shook his head. "I had no idea. Geena said you'd been injured, but—"

"I'm sure you didn't come here to discuss my well-being. Why do you think I know where she is?"

Lewis opened his soda and stared at the can as if marshaling his thoughts. He finally looked directly at Flynn. "I've been out of the country for a long time. When I returned last month, I came to Washington to visit Geena. We weren't always on good terms."

"You're much older."

"Yeah. Ten years. She's my half-sister. Different mothers." Lewis took a gulp of soda. "I last saw her five years ago in Spokane. In fact, she was with you at a friend's party."

Frowning, Flynn raised the footrest of his recliner. "Why didn't she introduce us?"

"She didn't know I was there. I…" Lewis pushed back among the cushions and seemed to regain his initial anger. His tone took on a harsher note. "When I went to the only address I had for her here in Tacoma—"

"Wait. She lived in Tacoma? Not Spokane?" Flynn shook his head.

"Guess you didn't know. Anyway, the apartment manager told me she'd left in a hurry with no forwarding address."

"When did she leave?"

"He said Christmas four years ago."

Flynn rubbed his chin. That was soon after she left him. "Go on."

"A neighbor saw me talking to the manager and said Geena asked her to keep a box of items for me if I showed up."

"What was in the box?"

"Letters. A diary." Lewis pointed to Flynn. "You have a lot of explaining to do, Mr. McCaul. Geena was afraid for her life. And you were her boyfriend. So, tell me, why was she afraid of you?"

"She wasn't." He grabbed the armrest. "Did she name me? What exactly did she say?"

"She wrote about threats, physical abuse—"

"Now, just a minute. I never hurt Geena. I'd never harm a woman. Ever." Flynn crushed his empty can. "None of this makes sense. What time period are you talking about? The Geena you're describing is not the woman I knew."

Lewis set his soda on the side table. "I have her diary right here." He pulled a small brown leatherbound book from his suit coat pocket and opened to a marked page. "Entry dated March, 2019, she wrote: *He called again last night. This time he threatened to go after my friends. I think it's time for me to leave.*"

Shaking his head Flynn held out his hand. "Can I see the diary?"

"No. I'm keeping it as evidence."

"Well, she can't be referring to me. At the date you mentioned, I was still in rehab. In Seattle. Geena broke up with me in July the previous year. I haven't seen her since."

Lewis stood and stepped to the mantel. "I don't understand."

Here it comes. Flynn cleared his throat. "Please sit down. This'll take a while. Let's start at the beginning." As Lewis returned to the sofa, Flynn gathered his words. Stick to the facts. Brief, to the point. No room for emotion. "I was injured June, 2018."

"An IED?"

"No. No. I'd already been honorably discharged by then. I was with my family to celebrate our parents' thirtieth anniversary." He chose to omit details about the intruder. "We'd rented a cabin and a faulty range exploded." Memories of the noise, the screams, the pain bombarded his mind. He swallowed. "My mom and dad were killed, and—"

"I'm sorry." Lewis leaned forward.

Flynn pointed to the scars on his left shoulder and arm. "Flying debris cut up my muscles pretty bad. Docs worked hard to save my leg. Surgeries, skin grafts, metal plates." He raised his left leg a fraction. "Now I live with nerve damage and associated pain. But at least I live. This is the new me, and Geena couldn't accept it. She visited me once, but I don't remember much, except her saying goodbye."

"Did she give you a reason?"

Flynn pursed his lips. Yeah, she did. And her words still stung. "Said she couldn't deal with the possibility of an amputation, of a husband with only one leg."

They sat in silence for a few moments, and then Lewis huffed out a sigh. "Sad to say, but that sounds like Geena. Putting someone else's needs above her own was never her strong suit."

At the time, Flynn had agreed with her reason for leaving. He didn't know how he was going to deal with the consequences of his injuries either. Now, in light of Lewis's assessment of Geena's character, he wondered if he'd allowed her physical beauty to overshadow her weaknesses.

"How'd you end up in Silverdale?" Lewis slid Geena's diary into his pocket.

"After rehab in Seattle, I returned to Spokane, but needed a change. I'd already been a realtor and heard about Thomas Tremaine and his interest in helping veterans. Meshed with my goal of locating affordable housing for vets." He didn't mean to give Lewis so much of his biography, but once he started, he couldn't stop. "Besides, my siblings live in the area."

The harsh lines on Lewis's face eased. He patted the pocket where he'd placed his sister's diary. "I guess I was mistaken about you. Geena must have been referring to someone else."

"Have you thought about hiring a private detective?"

"That's a good idea. I have business in Chicago

next week. I'll hire someone before I leave."

Flynn lowered the footrest and picked up the cane. "During my rehab, I called Geena a few times but she never answered. I accepted that as final. I'm sorry I don't have any information for you. Give me your contact details and I'll see what I can dig up."

With a grunt, Lewis stood and extracted a business card from his pocket. "I apologize for my initial attitude. I had no idea Geena had abandoned you."

Abandoned. Yeah, she'd done that. Although the hole in his heart had healed, he still had a difficult time trusting women who claimed to be romantically interested in him. Flynn took the card Lewis offered. All the talk about Geena had resurrected a slew of recollections, some pleasant, some agonizing. He stood and leaned on the cane. Time for the man who had the same brown eyes as his sister to leave.

"I'll be in touch if I discover anything."

"Thanks, Flynn. I'll see myself out."

After the door closed, Flynn set Lewis's card on the counter. He'd told the man he'd do some digging. Maybe contact a few old friends in Spokane. Flynn made his way to the kitchen and prepared supper. Soon spicy aromas swirled around him, and his thoughts strayed to his past with Geena. Places visited, dreams shared. While stirring the pan of marinera sauce, he remembered a keepsake box she'd given me. The US Marine's medallion decorated the lid of the dark brown oak, and green felt lined the eight-by-eight-inch interior. When unpacking in the condo, he'd used the heavy box as a bookend.

Flynn turned off the burner and hurried to his office. He sat on the bed, opened the box, and reviewed the contents he hadn't checked for several years. Unusual stones he'd collected. One silver cuff link. A key with a square of notebook paper taped to it. Flynn examined the key. He'd never seen it before. Too small for a door. Who had placed it in his box? And when? He removed the paper and unfolded it. Geena's handwriting scrawled across the page.

I'm leaving this key with you because you may need it one day to prove my innocence.

The paper drifted to the floor. Flynn stared at it. "What trouble are you in, Geena?"

Chapter 8

During the ten-mile drive to the Silverdale office the next morning, Jo ranted over Phil's message asking to meet, Serena's cruelty, and Max's chauvinism. Her jaw ached from clenching her teeth, and her shoulders strained against her rigid posture. Even the meeting with Danny and an hour-long stint in the gym the previous evening hadn't eased her anger and she'd had a miserable night. To add to her woes, she'd stepped on one of the little toys strewn across her bedroom carpet and bruised the instep of her right foot. She'd neglected to pick them up when she returned home the night before, and since she'd also trodden on the shoebox, the annoying things were now safely in a Ziplock bag. Under her bed. Lucia was still trying to find a working email for Charles Freeman.

She rubbed the tight muscles in her neck. All her personal items were in a box on her backseat. If Flynn didn't sanction her transfer today, she'd work out of her car, as she promised herself. She would not return to the Gig Harbor office. Ever.

After parking a few spaces from the office door, she turned off the engine, relaxed against the seat, and closed her eyes. Majestic scenes of snow-capped mountains and green forests etched in her memory from her recent bike ride helped focus her energy on the present, on proving to Flynn she would be an asset and not a liability.

Satisfied her anger and resentment had dissipated to acceptable levels, Jo exited her SUV and walked past the silver truck. The wheelchair hoist had been removed. She shrugged and entered the office, briefcase in hand and a smile on her lips. "Good morning, Brian. Is Flynn available?"

"Hey, Jo. Yeah. He's with Wesley. Hold on a sec. They might want you in on the conversation." He knocked on the door next to Flynn's office and opened it several inches. "Jo's here." Nodding, he turned and beckoned her. "Come in."

Shoulders back, she stepped through the doorway and sat in the chair beside Flynn. "Thanks for including me." She avoided his eyes and glanced at Wesley. The man seemed to have aged since yesterday. Lines creased his gaunt face and his eyebrows appeared as one thick, hairy line.

"I'm…I'm sorry for springing this on you, Jo. But I'm ready to transfer now, if that's okay with you. Flynn has agreed."

"Sure. Has something happened to Noah?"

"Yes and no. He's not happy with his new

placement. Although we discussed the move many times, he wants to come back home. And that's just not possible." Wesley wiped a hand across his face. "Iris can't handle him any longer, and we don't want to burden our older children with his care."

Flynn cleared his throat. "You don't have to justify your actions to us, Wes. Do what's best for your family. Take a few days off. Thomas won't mind, will he, Jo?"

"Of course not. I've already taken all my things from the office in Gig Harbor. What else can I do to help?"

Shaking his head, Wesley cuddled a stuffed black bear toy. "Nothing, thanks. Iris and I have to visit Noah and reassure him he's in a good place. I hope this new bear will lift his spirits. He's obsessed with bears." Tears filled his eyes. "Iris has a hard time getting about these days. She uses a walker and…and…"

Jo reached across the desk and took his hand. "I'm so sorry, Wesley. I didn't realize her MS had progressed that much."

"Iris has Multiple Sclerosis?" Flynn asked.

"Yeah." Jo squeezed Wesley's hand. "We'll leave you be for now." She picked up her purse and opened the door.

Flynn followed her out, cane in hand. "Let's chat in my office."

"Okay." She stopped by the reception desk. "Brian, please check on Wesley. See if he wants a cup of coffee."

He nodded. "Will do."

Purse on the floor beside a chair, Jo sat and waited for Flynn to settle behind his desk. He limped more than yesterday, and he grimaced a couple of times.

"Before we discuss your move, I need to apologize for my curtness toward you. It's not an excuse, but I was tired and in pain."

Now would be a good time to ask for details, but she didn't have to.

"I don't know how much Thomas has shared, but I have severe nerve damage in my left leg, and I need a brace to help me walk more normally. Yesterday, the brace rubbed blisters and I'm not wearing it today. Hence, the cane. For stability." He gestured as if washing his hands. "Now that's out of the way, tell me about your clients. I know you often work with the property management team."

"Before I do that, I have a favor. Can I work out of the conference room until Wesley's office is available?"

"Yes. You can store your belongings in there too."

"Thanks. I don't have much. Mostly contractor files, which I know we need to discuss." She leaned forward. "I'll be working on Nelda Yates's property in Holly when the sheriff releases it." She explained the reason she had to wait.

"The bomb squad! Have you heard anything about the scarf?"

"No. I hope it wasn't Rosie's blood."

"How much work are we talking about?"

"A considerable amount. Drywall repair, painting of all the bedrooms and bathrooms. I want the bold, floral wallpaper removed from the bathrooms. Re—"

"You're not a fan of wallpaper?"

"Not bold patterns, and certainly not flowers. I like my blooms outside, on stems, on shrubs and trees, as nature intended. I don't even like artificial flowers."

"Duly noted."

Jo had no idea what to make of his quizzical expression. She frowned and continued with her list. "Replace carpets or install hardwood floors. Tiles replaced in one bathroom. Some windowpanes. Instead of fixing the old barn, I suggest it be demolished. And landscaping."

"We, that is, Elrod Construction, my brother-in-law's company, can handle everything except the landscape."

"No problem. I've worked with a couple of reputable companies." All the while she talked, she paid attention to Flynn's face. He tried to hide a wince now and again. Probably the nerve pain he mentioned. "I have other clients who just signed a contract to rent their home in Brownsville. Garland and Velma Adair. We toured the property, and I took a load of photos. Other than shampooing the carpets and mowing the lawn, the place is ready to advertise. Have you met Eileen Trask?"

He shook his head.

"She handles all the paperwork in our property management division. Advertising, vetting renters, contracts, collection of funds, et cetera. Naturally, she works at the Gig Harbor office."

"When you bring in your files, let me check out the contractors. See if Stan uses any of them."

"I have one other potential client." Jo outlined Serena's handling of the Napier's deal.

"That was very unprofessional of her. Do you know why?"

Jo rolled her eyes. She could spend the next hour theorizing, but she only said, "I have my suspicions which I won't share at this point. Anyway, two days ago, Scott Napier gave my name to friends of theirs who also want to purchase a home on Bainbridge Island. I haven't heard from them yet. When Nelda's house is available, I'll be busy, but until them, I'm all yours." She regretted the last words as soon as they slipped over her lips, and she gulped.

For the first time in their acquaintance, Flynn actually smiled at her. His gray eyes lit up and the lines of his square jaw softened. "I'll remember that, Miss Tremaine."

"I'll set up in the conference room now." Cheeks heating, she stood.

"Brian can help you."

She didn't reply and left the office. Once in the hall, she drew in a breath. Except for her poor choice of words, the meeting went well. Better than she'd expected.

For the next hour, Jo sorted through her files, weeding out personal notes, old lists of needed repairs, and contractors Tremaine Realty no longer used. Close to eleven o'clock, she had arranged the remaining files in groups and poked her head in Flynn's office.

He acknowledged her presence with another smile.

"The files are ready."

"I'll be there in five minutes."

Jo waited for Brian to end his telephone conversation, then asked, "How's Wesley?"

"He's packing up. But I think he's okay. He had a long talk with Iris and seemed to be more positive afterward."

"Thanks." She returned to the conference room and Flynn joined her minutes later. When she offered him a chocolate from her bowl, he declined, but she nibbled on a square. They spent a half-hour reviewing the contractors and found three Stan used.

"We'll set up a schedule when you're allowed back at Nelda's." Flynn checked his watch. "I have a couple of errands before I meet a client for lunch." He pulled a folded piece of paper from his pocket. "Look this over for me, please. I…I'll be teaching self-defense classes once a week. What do you think of my advertisement?"

The notice was succinct, all pertinent details included. She handed it back to him. "It caught my attention."

"Good. You can attend anytime." He eased out of

the chair. "Work here as long as you like. I'm glad you'll be on our team." His cane tapped and his left shoe clomped as he walked down the hall.

Jo leaned back and sighed. In spite of his initial terseness, she might enjoy working with Errol Flynn McCaul. He certainly wouldn't complain about her boots.

Her phone rang and she searched for it in her voluminous purse. Kendy always teased her about the size, but she needed every last item in it. The screen displayed the Kitsap County Sheriff Department logo. "Joanna Tremaine speaking."

"This is Deputy Frances Gordon. Two things. We've released Mrs. Yates's home. You can return anytime, and—"

"Can you share any details with me?" Jo figured her question wouldn't be answered, but she had to ask.

"The blood on the scarf was human, but we found no other evidence of foul play. Authorities are not ready to reveal anything about your other discovery."

"I understand. What was the second thing?"

"The email you provided for Charles Freeman is not correct. My message bounced back. Please resend."

"I took it straight from his rental agreement with the other property management company, but I will check." Jo ended the call then opened her laptop and searched for the Freeman file her father and forwarded. She had provided the deputy the correct email. To be doubly sure, she emailed Lucia, explained the situation and asked her to verify the contact details with the previous company. If they couldn't contact Freeman, then Jo couldn't return the shoebox she'd found. His loss.

Time for lunch. She stopped at Ethan's office where he and Brian were eating tuna sandwiches, by the unmistakable…bouquet. "Is Wesley still here?"

Brian shook his head. "He left about five minutes ago to fetch boxes for his stuff. Said he'll be out of his office later today."

"Thanks. I'm going to see what fancy eateries you have around here." Jo donned her sunglasses and strolled through the parking lot intent on walking to a strip mall nearby. A man dressed in dark pants and shirt spoke to Wesley who stood beside his car and held the stuffed bear. The stranger's bald head and lean physique poked at a memory, and when he gave her a quick glance, she recognized Lewis Pierce. What business did he have with Wesley? Pumping him for information about Flynn?

Jo shrugged. Questions to be asked when Wesley returned. She continued her search for a meal and as she turned a corner, enticing aromas of curry wafted past her nose. Yep. An Indian restaurant would fit the bill. Her phone rang and she answered while standing at the glass doors.

"Miss Jo, this is Gerry. Gerry Collins. Hope I'm not bothering you."

"Nope. How can I help you?"

"This might sound presumptuous, but will you join

me for lunch?"

Certainly not what she expected. She'd anticipated he'd share the name of a prospective client. "All right. Where and when?"

"Silverdale, in about five minutes."

"Okaaaay. What restaurant?"

"How about North Indian Cuisine?"

Jo lowered her phone and pivoted. Gerry stood on the sidewalk about ten yards away. She slipped the phone into her purse and set her hands on her hips.

He sauntered toward her. "Hi."

"What are you doing here?" *Really, Jo. You couldn't think of a better question?* She lowered her arms.

"I wanted to see you again and instead of a cold call, I decided meeting in person would, um, convince you I was serious. Found out you worked in the Silverdale realty office. Stopped by and Brian told me you were looking for a restaurant." He smiled and cocked his head.

The words in his first sentence took a stroll through her mind. He wanted to see *her* again. No real estate involved. "I love Indian food."

He held the door open for her. Max had never been so gallant.

Chapter 9

Tossing and catching the small key over and over, Flynn reviewed a dozen scenarios of what Geena's note might mean. How was he supposed to help her if he didn't know anything about the key?

He huffed out a breath and set the little object on his desk. His lunch meeting resulted in the client contracting Tremaine Realty to locate a home in the Poulsbo area. They were scheduled to meet again the next week. And he'd displayed his flyer in three grocery stores, in the hall the church used for their Sunday services and provided the details of his classes to the Kitsap County Sheriff's Department.

The front door opened, and Jo entered. Flynn called for her to join him. He cast a quick glance at her and did a double take. Her green eyes sparkled, and she seemed relaxed, happy. In previous contact with her, she'd conducted herself professionally, assertive at times, but always aloof. Working with her would not be dull. "You look pleased with yourself."

She proffered a one-sided smile and sat. "I am. I

have many reasons to be thankful I'm at this office. I won't bore you with all of them, but I received a call from Tony and Helen Underwood, friends of a former client who are looking for a home on Bainbridge Island. And Nelda's house has been released. I love making broken things whole, restoring beauty from ugly."

"That's great." He sensed she had more to share. "And?"

Running her hand through her wild, auburn curls, she leaned back. "And I met a…friend for lunch."

No expert on woman, but Flynn would bet Jo liked the friend. *Too personal.* He cleared his throat. "Wesley is almost ready to load up his truck. You can move into the office later today."

"Good. I hope working closer to home will ease his stress." She balanced her purse on her knees. "How do you want to proceed with Nelda's property?"

"Stan has a checklist where you can document all needed repairs in detail. I'll forward a copy to you."

"I have multiple photos, too."

"Include those. Then he and I will decide on a foreman, who might be me since it's a Tremaine property, and we'll schedule the contractors."

"You really do work for Stan?"

"Yep. I like to keep up my skills, get my hands dirty. Once we—"

"Why do you have a locker key from my gym on your desk?" She frowned.

"This one belongs to Geena." Finally, an answer.

"Where's the gym?"

"How come you have her key? I thought…never mind."

He explained where he'd found the key and the note attached.

"That's a dramatic statement. Innocent of what?"

Flynn shrugged. "I've had no contact with her for four years."

"My gym is in Bremerton, but they have several locations." She picked up the key and examined it. "My key has the letter *B* etched on it. This key has a *G* which could indicate Gig Harbor. Check online to see where the other branches are."

"What's the name?"

"*Bene Vivere.*"

"Really?"

She giggled. "Latin for *Live Well.*"

Flynn entered the name in a web search and found five gyms in the franchise. "Bremerton, Olympia, two in Tacoma, and yes, Gig Harbor."

"Why would Geena use a facility in Gig Harbor?"

"My question, exactly. Lewis said she moved from Spokane to Tacoma, so why not use a gym there?" He rubbed his aching left knee. If only he could ease the ache in his brain as easily. He thumped the desk. "This means she knows where I live and left the key in my new condo. Recently. She wouldn't obtain a key to the Gig Harbor location and take it all the way to my place in Spokane before I moved."

"It's strange that she chose Gig Harbor when Bremerton is closer to Silverdale."

"I'm puzzled by the whole situation." He leaned back and rocked.

"By the way, as I was leaving the office earlier, I saw Lewis talking to Wesley. Any idea why?"

Flynn shook his head. Was the guy stalking him? "I'll call the Gig Harbor location and ask…no, bad idea."

"I agree. They wouldn't reveal member details over the phone. However, the code on the key indicates her locker number."

He had no pressing business and hoped Jo didn't either. "I'm going to visit the gym. Can you come with me? Geena gave me the key for a reason. I have to find out if she left anything in her locker. Do you get more than one key?"

"Yes, if you pay extra."

"I'll drive. My truck gives me lots of leg room." Flynn notified Brian of their plans and grabbed his cane. He could walk without it, but that increased the likelihood of him tripping. Falling flat on his face. Not in front of Jo.

During the half-hour drive, Flynn wanted to find out more about her, and asked a question he thought would facilitate friendship. "I believe you spent your vacation riding cross-country for hundreds of miles. Isn't it dangerous? I mean, you do ride with a group, right?" Why'd he add the questions? His attempt at comradery just fell flat. Jo's quick glance his way confirmed he'd gone too far.

"I belong to the Peninsula Bike and Hike Club. Several of us make a long trip once a year. We like to ride together a couple of times a month."

He grimaced at her hard tone.

"We never ride alone. We carry spare parts, SAT phones, and each of us knows how to make repairs, fix tires. It's not like we try to cross the Sahara." Arms folded, she stared straight ahead.

"I'm sorry, I didn't mean to insinuate you were amateurs. Just concerned about your, um, safety."

Jo didn't respond right away, and Flynn gave himself a virtual thump on the head. His need to protect people in his life had disrupted his ability to interact normally with a peer again.

"Thanks for your concern, but I can take care of myself."

"I have no doubt." He shifted in the seat. "Can we forget my overbearing attitude and remarks, and return to the ride? How many rode with you? Men, women?"

"Four of us went this time. Danny De La Cruz, and married couple Emma and Vic Garnett."

Two men in the group. He applauded his prudence for not saying the thought out loud and cleared his throat. "Have you always been interested in long distance biking?"

"I ran track in middle school, high school, and college, but switched to bike-riding after, um, later."

Her arms relaxed and her voice held a note of amusement. "I love the adrenaline rush, the outdoors, the wind in my face. I joined this this club when I began working for my folks, a year ago. You should—" She touched his cane wedged beside his seat. "Sorry."

"No problem. I can ride a bike, but not for miles on end. I have an idea. Get a tandem and I can be your backseat driver." Why'd he spout those words? Maybe in an effort to wipe away his previous gaff. He focused on the road and ignored the heat rising up his neck.

A soft giggle, then an all-out belly laugh. A surprising response. He glanced at Jo who held her stomach as if it hurt.

"What's so funny?"

She almost choked trying to breathe. "The picture of you on a tandem."

"Why?"

"Have you seen one up close?"

"Are you insinuating I'm fat?"

"No. But you are...bulky. You might not fit between the saddle and the handlebars."

He shook his head and held his hand over his heart. "I'm mortified. But in all seriousness, when I ride a stationary bike for any length of time, my nerve pain increases." Who kept introducing topics he wanted to avoid?

"How is your foot today?"

Exactly where he didn't want the conversation to go, but he replied, "Better, thanks. I need a different brace or thicker socks." Enough with the sharing. He couldn't blame her for asking the inevitable.

"How'd you injure your leg?"

Omitting the nitty-gritty and therefore the emotional undertones, he described the accident and subsequent rehab. "Although the foot-drop and residual nerve pain are annoying, at least I kept my leg."

"That's a positive."

"Yeah." He had to turn the conversation in a safer direction. "So, tell me why you prefer Jo to Joanna?"

She sat bolt-upright and gave him a disapproving glare.

Oops. Not so positive. "I'm curious."

"Since you are part of the business family, I'll tell you more than you bargained for. Apparently, Mom's ultrasound indicated I was a boy. Dad was ecstatic and wanted to name me Joseph, to honor his grandfather. Well, both parents were surprised when I arrived. Twenty-one inches long, red-headed, but a girl." She folded her arms again and looked straight ahead. "Dad was probably disappointed, but he's never treated me any different than my sister. Mother, on the other hand, seemed to blame me. She wanted to give Dad a son. We've been at odds all my life."

Flynn mentally compared petite Anita to Jo and shook his head. "You—"

"There's more. When Dad completed the birth certificate, he decided not to give me the name Mother chose. I'll love him forever for that decision. Instead, he combined his grandfather's name and her name. Hence, Joanna."

"What name did Anita choose?"

"Candace." Jo harrumphed. "Can you imagine me with the nickname Candy? I was teased all through elementary school because of my height. And redder than red hair. Add Candy to the mix, and life would have been unbearable. I was anything but sweet."

Flynn wanted to pat her shoulder, but changed his mind when she continued.

"I learned to defend myself, physically, but the words...cut deep." She blew out a breath. "By middle school, some boys had caught up with me in inches and I won many track meets, so the teasing stopped. But if you value your life, never call me Joanna." She faced him and a slow smile graced her face.

"I won't." Tough childhood, but she appeared to have risen above the criticism. He almost said as much to her, but he held his tongue when a billboard caught his attention, and he took the exit for Purdy.

"This isn't the way."

"I know, but I want to check out..." He parked in front of a single-story motel block. "That."

"Why? Is Tremaine Realty in the market to purchase a motel?"

"No, but I am." He withdrew his phone from his pocket and entered the contact details for the seller. "One of my goals is to facilitate affordable housing for veterans. Your dad agreed to partner with me in this endeavor." Opening his door, he looked at Jo. "Let's check it out." Cane in hand, he walked toward the building.

"A worthy goal. These units would probably make suitable accommodation for single people. Bathrooms, kitchenettes." She approached a wall and poked at peeling paint.

"Yeah. And there's a bus stop on the corner and enough yard for dogs. Many veterans have dogs."

"That's important. Taking care of another life helps people take care of themselves. I'd love to have a dog, but not in my small apartment."

Noting the sympathy in her tone, Flynn stuck his hands on his hips. He'd been on the lookout for such a project and circled the building to take photos. Now to convince Thomas.

Back in the pickup, Jo gave him directions to the gym where he found a spot to park a few yards from the entrance. He unbuckled his seatbelt, but she held out a hand in front of him.

"Hold on. I don't think you should go in."

"But I…" His earlier doubt of her ability fresh on his mind, he said, "Okay. What's your plan?"

"I'll pretend to be a friend who needs to leave something in Geena's locker. You won't be welcome in the woman's area. What do you have I can use?"

"Check the glovebox."

She pulled the latch, rummaged inside, and removed a Bible. "You keep one in your car, too?"

"Why not? Here's Geena's key."

Slipping the Bible into her purse and palming the key, she exited the truck and entered the facility.

The reflective glass prevented him from watching her, and since she didn't come out right away meant her ploy had been successful. While he waited, he checked his phone for messages. Brian had a question about a new client. Melanie invited him for a cookout on Saturday. He responded, but kept an eye on the glass doors. Jo had been gone ten minutes, and Flynn drummed his thumbs on the steering wheel. Fifteen minutes and he was ready to climb out.

At last, she strolled toward him, a gym bag slung over her shoulder along with her purse.

"Success?"

She climbed into the truck. "Yup. It took a while for me to convince the receptionist to allow me access to Geena's locker. Of course, I couldn't tell her I didn't know the number, but I have a pretty good idea how to read the code on each key. However, when I located the section, I had to wait for a couple of chatty teens to leave before I could try the key."

"And the bag is Gena's?"

"Yeah. Your name is pinned to the strap." She handed him the bag.

Inside were workout clothes and a cosmetics bag. Faint whiffs of her citrusy perfume hit his nose. He ignored the instant pang and the T-shirt and yoga pants and opened the pouch. Among the lipsticks and mascara tube he found a digital tape recorder and removed it. He clicked the play button, but nothing happened. "Why leave a blank recorder?"

"Could be the batteries are dead."

He flipped open the back panel, and sure enough, no batteries.

"We passed a convenience store on the previous block."

"Good idea." While driving down the road, he asked, "Did you learn anything useful from the receptionist?"

"Could be important details. Geena recently transferred membership from Tacoma to Gig Harbor, and she was last in two weeks ago."

About the time he moved into his new condo. He frowned as he parked. "I'll go in." He purchased a pack of AAA batteries and hurried back to the pickup.

Jo took the package from his fumbling fingers and inserted two batteries into the recorder. She passed it to him. "You do the honors."

He turned it on, his gut muscles tensing. Static then Geena's voice, "I don't have much time for explanations, Flynn. First, I'm sorry for abandoning you. If you're listening to me then it means Lewis found you. He and I have never been close, that's why I didn't mention him to you. Please, please, don't tell him you have this message."

A click as if she stopped recording. Flynn hit pause and took the opportunity to look at Jo.

She hiked a shoulder. "Sounds like her brother is an unsavory character."

"Maybe so, but I didn't get that vibe when we met." He pushed play again.

"I found out you worked for Tremaine Realty." Geena chuckled for a brief second. "You used Amy from your old office in Spokane as a reference. She told me. Anyway, my gym bag has a false bottom. I hid a journal there. Don't touch the envelope inside."

Flynn paused the recording as Jo picked up the bag, located the hidden compartment, and removed the book.

"Let me have it." He thumbed through the blank pages until he came to a cream-colored envelope which had Geena's name scrawled on it. As instructed, he didn't touch it, but closed the book and, his gut muscles doing calisthenics, he hit play.

"Lewis sent me the letter. Pushed it under my door. Therefore, my DNA and his are on it. Important facts. Six months ago, he'd asked me to meet him at a lawyer's office where we were supposed to discuss an inheritance of some kind. When I arrived in the parking garage, I found Lewis standing over the body of the lawyer. He had blood on his hands.

"Lewis swore me to secrecy. Claimed he didn't kill the lawyer, but he'd had an argument with him the previous day which the assistant overheard. We've only recently discovered an uncle left most of his fortune to me. If for some reason I'm arrested for this murder, please give the envelope and this recording to someone high up in the police department. Lewis is an ex-cop and has many friends on the force and he knows how to manipulate evidence. Under no circumstances let Lewis know you have it."

Jo placed the journal back in the compartment and zipped up the gym bag.

Geena continued. "The lawyer's death never made it to the news. I've often thought Lewis staged it all to scare me, blackmail me. Maybe the inheritance was a ruse because I've heard nothing more about it. Don't try to find me. I'm hiding out. Oh, and get a security system for your condo. I broke in easily to hide the key in the box I gave you. I knew if Lewis contacted you and asked about me, you'd check the box. Which you did. Take care."

Flynn turned off the recording and leaned against the seat. "Poor Geena. She sounds terrified. We must hide her bag and keep its location secret from Lewis at all costs." He handed Jo the recorder. "Why would Geena hide the letter in a blank journal? It appeared new. Which reminds me. When Lewis came to see me, he read from a diary he said was Geena's. He wouldn't let me see it, and it appeared to be new, too. Strange thing is, I never saw Geena with a diary or journal. Maybe he lied about it."

"But we know this recording is genuine."

"It's her voice all right. I wonder..." Unable to complete the sentence, he closed his eyes. He had no idea how Jo would react to his praying. He didn't care. "Father, God, please protect Geena and help me in my quest to provide housing for my buddies. In Jesus' name. Amen."

Chapter 10

Living in an apartment with no garage caused Jo headaches at times. Although she'd rented a storage unit for her collection of bikes and excess furniture, she longed for the day she could afford a house. However, the unit served as a good hiding place for Geena's gym bag. Jo locked the door, scanned the surroundings to make sure Lewis was not in sight, then drove to the Silverdale office.

Flynn's questions the previous day concerning her safety on her cross-country trip had come out of left field. At first, she thought Mother had asked him to convince her to quit the club, but he'd quickly apologized and hadn't stressed the point. However, she needed to guard against any man who attempted to control her life. With good intensions or not. Considering her recent breakup with Max, she had no interest in searching for a man, a husband, anytime soon. Gerry was fun to be with, but not her type at all. She scratched her temple. Did she have a type?

Upon entering the office, Brian informed her Flynn

and Ethan were both out with clients and offered to make her a cup of coffee. Jo accepted the cup and set about organizing her space. Which didn't take long. While completing the spreadsheet for Stan, Tony Underwood called to say he and Helen were ready to view homes. Jo had located several properties on Bainbridge Island that met their criteria. Serena would not snatch *this* sale from her. Jo arranged to meet them that afternoon in Poulsbo where they were presently renting.

Could her day get any better? Yup. Gerry stopped by with an office-warming gift—a potted pothos ivy. "Thank you. I hope I can keep it alive."

"It's easy to take care of, even in a window-less office."

That was the only aspect of her previous office she missed. "Did you come all the way from Holly to deliver the plant?"

"And to ask you out. Are you doing anything exciting this Saturday?"

"No. I don't consider laundry much fun."

"How about we go for a ride?"

"As in horses, car, bike?"

"Bike. Do you have more than one? If not, I could borrow—"

"You can use my Canyon Strive. And I have an extra helmet." She grinned. "What prompted this particular invitation?"

"The description of your vacation ride." He stood

and shoved his hands into his pockets. "You decide where we'll go, but please have pity on me. I haven't ridden in a long time. Call me later and let me know where, when." He beamed a bright smile at her. "See ya."

Jo touched a leaf on the plant and sighed. Riding with Gerry would probably be a blast and the gift showed his thoughtfulness, but when would he reveal his true colors? In her experience, every man she'd ever liked had disappointed her.

Burying old memories, Jo forwarded the spreadsheet to Stan and Flynn. She was keen to begin the work on Nelda's house. In the meantime, she checked on the status of the Adair's rental property and printed out the specs for the three homes the Underwoods would visit. She'd already sent the showing requests and had received confirmation for the times. Eager sellers accepted most requests. A good sign for Jo and the clients.

Later, while she ate lunch in the conference room, Flynn returned and joined her at the table and set his cane on the floor.

"I haven't had time to review the spreadsheet, but Stan says you did a great job. He knows exactly what needs to be done, and he approved me as the foreman. I'm looking forward to working on Nelda's house. Will you be available to visit tomorrow?"

She sipped her water and nodded. "Unless the Underwoods want to see more houses. I'm taking them to Bainbridge at two this afternoon."

Scooting back from the table, he placed his left foot on his right knee and rubbed his ankle.

"No new brace yet?"

"It has to be custom-made and might be ready later this week. But for now, I plod along with my trusty aid." He set his foot on the floor and leaned back. "Change of subject. Melanie, my sister, invited me to a cook-out Saturday. Would you like to come?"

Two invites in as many hours. From two handsome men. Jo rolled her eyes. It didn't take much to please her. But to be honest, she'd rather have gone with Flynn. "I'd love to meet your sister, but I have a…" she bit back the word *date*, "a riding excursion planned."

Was that a flash of disappointment in his eyes? "Next time." He picked up his cane, ready to stand.

"Wait. Did you talk to Dad about the motel?"

An instant smile hid whatever emotion she'd noticed. "Yes. Obviously, I can't afford the place, and he doesn't want to commit Tremaine Realty to a large financial outlay. However, he is so resourceful. He suggested several charitable organizations that work for veterans who may contribute. Of course, I know of some, but in the past, my pleas for assistance have gone unanswered. He also mentioned large corporations who donate funds to worthy causes. Many for a tax write-off, but if the money is green, I'll take advantage of their generosity."

"Yeah. Dad has contacts all over Washington State.

He's been in business a long time and has earned a positive reputation."

"I have to write all the letters requesting assistance, but that's a chore I'll gladly tackle. Using Thomas as a reference should get me results."

"When it comes time to renovate, count me in. I'm handy with a paint brush and will offer my decorating tips free of charge."

Flynn stood and balanced himself, one hand on his cane, the other on the table. "I'll keep that in mind. I hope the Underwoods find a home today."

"Me, too. I'll let you know what happens."

"Thanks." He pivoted and limped down the hall.

Jo cleaned away her salad bowl and freshened up for her meeting with Tony and Helen. Details of the homes selected in hand, she headed to Poulsbo. A rain shower slowed traffic, but she arrived on time and the clients rode in her SUV to the island. Although continued rain obscured views across the Puget Sound, the Underwoods were suitably impressed with the second house. Not only did the property suit their needs, it was a block over from their friends, Scott and Donna Napier. Tony and Helen returned home, assuring Jo that after discussing details with their financial team, they would submit an offer.

Preening just a little, Jo entered the Silverdale office and shared her news with Flynn.

"Congratulations." He stood and shook her hand. "A sale Serena can't snatch from you."

His mention of the blonde's name dampened Jo's enthusiasm a tad.

"Keep me updated. Do you have anything on your calendar for tomorrow?" Seated again, he opened his laptop.

"Nothing definite."

"Good. I'm meeting one of the contractor's at Nelda's house in the morning." He looked up at her, eyebrows raised. "Can you join us?"

"Of course. Jackson Reed from Yards Galore Landscapers will come one day next week to check out the gardens and give me a quote." Forgetting his previous ill-chosen questions, the thought of working on site with Flynn set Jo's heart aflutter. "I need to get started on the paperwork for the Underwoods." She lowered her head to hide the flush she felt creeping into her cheeks. *Chill, Jo.*

Flynn snagged his jacket from the back of his chair, grabbed his cane, and pointed to the door. "See you in the morning. I'm installing a security system at my condo this evening."

"No more clandestine visits from Geena." Jo stepped out of his office but not before she noticed Flynn's frown.

"Considering the trouble Lewis is causing her, I don't want either of them near my place."

Jo deposited her purse and briefcase in her office, sank into her chair, and munched on a piece of chocolate. Flynn had shown concern for Geena's wellbeing after they'd listened to her recording. Even prayed for her. Jo recalled the Bible she'd found in his glovebox and the one displayed on his desk. If ever she needed spiritual guidance to get her life back on track, she'd approach her boss who seemed to practice the Christian principles she'd been exposed to in her youth.

Twenty minutes on the treadmill and fifteen on the step-climber at the gym that afternoon helped enhance Jo's positive frame of mind.

~

Dressed in a tangerine-colored top, and, ignoring Mother's snide comment, another pair of brown slacks and her comfortable boots, Jo drove to Nelda Yates's property. She retrieved the key from the lock box and waved to Flynn as he pulled in beside her vehicle and parked.

He strolled toward the oak doors while surveying the grand proportions of the house. "Wow. Such a magnificent place to be damaged by renters." He shook his head. "Show me around."

Jo averted her eyes from his torso covered in a well-fitting gray T-shirt. No wonder his sports coat had looked a size too small. She cleared her throat and, referring to the spreadsheet on her iPad, stammered her way through the list of repairs needed downstairs.

"Very thorough. Good job." He smiled and leaned on his cane.

Jo basked in his praise for a moment. "Do you want to see the mess upstairs?"

"Not yet." A vehicle door slammed. Flynn turned toward the open front doors. "We've hired Strategic Repairs as our general contractor. My brother-in-law has used the company for years. That should be Landon Hunt, one of their supervisors."

A stocky man with shoulder-length black hair knocked on the door and entered. "Hey, Flynn. Good to work with you again."

Jo extended her hand. "Joanna Tremaine." She met Landon's firm grip with one of her own.

Another knock on the door. This time the man was at least six-foot, ruddy complexion, and his high forehead led to thinning blond hair.

"Stan. I wasn't expecting you." Flynn turned to Jo. "My brother-in-law."

"Good to meet the person who did such a thorough job on the repairs spreadsheet."

Again, Jo shook hands and beamed. "I hope Tremaine Realty will send lots of business your way."

"Let's start upstairs." Flynn grabbed the banister. "You three go ahead. I'll catch up."

Landon was also impressed with the details Jo provided. After they returned to the kitchen, Flynn, Stan, and Landon discussed a schedule for the repairs. Glad to be relieved of this chore, Jo strolled outside to check on the barn. The ammo cans and tarpaulin had been removed and only trash lay strewn about.

Hearing a soft whine, she stepped out the door and spied the little dog ten yards from her. He held up one paw and didn't scamper away. She spoke in hushed tones and approached him. He cowered and whimpered. No wonder. Quills protruded from his muzzle, neck, and front leg. Porcupines were a rare sight in this part of Washington, so where had the animal encountered one? The dog allowed her to pick him up. She could feel his ribs and her heart melted. Cradling him carefully, she rushed to the house and called to Flynn from the back door. "Please locate the nearest veterinary clinic."

He took one look at the dog and nabbed his phone. A few seconds later, he said, "Back in Silverdale. Do you want me to go with you?"

"Yes. I can't hold him and drive."

"I'll help you into my truck." He secured her seatbelt, careful to avoid the animal.

"You poor little thing. I don't know how people can abandon pets."

"Did the previous renters leave their dog behind?"

"I don't think so. He's the same mutt I saw previously. The one who deposited the bloody scarf. Probably a stray."

"Melanie mentioned they'd like to get a dog for their kids. I'll tell her about this guy."

Flynn's sensitivity to the wounded creature sat well with her, as did his concern for the veterans he was trying to help. When she received her hefty commission from the Underwoods' purchase, she'd donate a chunk to his motel venture.

The trip seemed to take an agonizingly long time. Flynn helped Jo out of the truck, and she explained the situation to the receptionist. Soon, a tech took the dog to an examination room.

After leaving her contact information and assurances she'd pay for the treatment, Jo returned to Flynn's pickup.

He reversed out of the parking lot. "I gather you like dogs."

"One day I'd love to own a house on a large piece of property so I can take in rescue dogs. Big, little. Young, old. We could never have pets when I was a kid. Too many moves to military housing."

"We always had at least one dog. I have a similar desire to own a large property so I can keep military dogs who outgrow their useful careers."

"What a great idea. Maybe we…never mind. We're almost at Nelda's." Jo uncrossed her legs and bumped her knee on the glovebox, bringing to mind the Bible she'd found. "Why do you keep a Bible in your vehicle?"

"So people like you will ask."

"Like me?" Jo wasn't sure if she should be offended or not.

"You know, a good person. But—"

"That's the big question, isn't it? But, what? I no longer believe? I'm the lost sheep?"

"Are you? I'd love to help you find your way back to the Shepherd."

She gazed out the window until he parked next to her SUV in Nelda's driveway. Climbing out of the truck, she shook her head. She'd have to confess to her parents first before she could consider a change in her spiritual life. "I'm going back to Silverdale. You and Landon and Stan can complete your plans and let me know my role."

Jo Stumbled to her car. Yeah. She was stumbling through life. Had been since Phil's betrayal, many years ago.

Chapter 11

Excited about beginning repairs on Nelda's house, Flynn thumped one hand on the steering wheel in time to the beat of a song playing on his phone. Landon would send the first team over Monday. Carpet removal, cracked glass panes replaced, sheet rock installation, electrician.

He frowned and his hand stilled. Jo and her response to his statement about the Bible sat heavy on his heart. He prayed he hadn't turned her away. What happened to cause her coldness toward religion? Flynn knew she'd been raised in a Christian home, and he was now aware of the difficult relationship she had with her mother, but surely something else had negatively affected her. Maybe as they worked together on the house, he could broach the subject again.

Brian and Ethan had just sat down to eat lunch when Flynn entered the Silverdale office.

"Come join us." Brian waved to him from the conference room.

"Thanks." Flynn reheated his leftover lasagna in the

small breakroom, then sat at the table with the men. He knew quite a bit about Brian, but had not had the opportunity to spend much time with Ethan. The quiet-spoken man had a good sales history and had been with the company since graduating from university ten years ago. "Any plans for a summer vacation, Ethan?" A good place to begin.

"No. We usually take a break in the fall and visit family in Florida. My in-laws have a house right on the beach in Pensacola, and the boys love to spend time with their grandparents building sandcastles and collecting shells."

Turns out, the boys were four-year-old twins. The conversation soon veered to Brian and his wife's pregnancy, leaving Flynn feeling like he was missing out on something important.

Having finished his meal, he picked up his empty container and asked, "Have you seen Jo recently?"

Brian nodded. "She came in about an hour and a half ago, but left again after receiving a phone call. She didn't say where she was going."

Flynn had hoped to revisit their conversation, but maybe Jo would be more receptive after a cooling off period. He worked in his office the rest of the afternoon, and the next morning, took the ferry from Kingston to Edmonds, north of Seattle.

Stan and Melanie lived a short drive from the ferry dock. Their children, Haley and Pam, were excited to see their uncle and loved to hang on his outstretched arms while he walked like a robot. As they had grown, he could hold them for shorter and shorter periods of time.

"Okay, girls. That's enough. I'm getting too old for this." Flynn exaggerated gasped-in breaths and sank onto a stool at the kitchen counter.

Haley stood beside him and patted his shoulder. "Uncle Flynn, when are you going to have children?"

"Honey, that's not a question you should be asking." Melanie tsked as she pulled a container of her signature baked beans from the oven.

Flynn ignored the notes of molasses and bacon filling the kitchen and frowned at Haley. "Why do you want to know?"

"Well, my friend has seven cousins and I have none. She said the only way I can get cousins is if my uncles or aunts marry and have kids. Since Daddy has no brothers or sisters, that leaves you and Uncle Ian. And he's too busy in the Marines."

Melanie looked at Flynn across the counter and raised her eyebrows. He shook his head at his sister then ruffled Haley's strawberry-blonde hair. "I don't have a girlfriend, but when I find a woman I want to marry, I'll be sure to tell you."

"Okay." Seemingly satisfied, she snatched a potato chip from a bowl near Flynn's elbow.

"Take those outside and help Daddy set the table." Melanie shooed the girls toward the French doors. "We're almost ready to eat."

Right in the middle of the meal, rain sent them all scurrying inside. Settled at the dining table, Melanie continued the conversation she'd begun. "Sounds like you made the right decision to move from Spokane. Stan said he met Joanna, the boss's daughter. What's it like working with her?"

"Jo, she prefers Jo." Flynn took a gulp of water. "She's—"

"A tall redhead. Knows her stuff."

"Hush, honey." Melanie elbowed her husband. "I want Flynn's opinion."

"Um, she's a good agent, works hard. Intelligent, and I'm happy she's in our office." He finally raised his gaze from his plate and looked at his sister. "Great meal."

"Is that all you have to say about her? Is she married, single? Does she have a boyfriend?"

He raised his hand in a stop gesture. "Quit the interrogation. Jo is single."

"One last question. Is she attractive? My sweet husband said she was tall and had red hair. Usually when he describes a woman he adds pretty or something similar." Melanie tilted her head. "Well?"

Flynn recalled the first time he'd seen Jo. Although dealing with pain and worrying about his presentation, of course he was aware of her height, but he'd also noticed how her hair emphasized her green eyes. How her smile softened her angular features. Her lips... *Stop*. "Jo is attractive, and she has a kind heart. Just yesterday she found a stray dog at Nelda Yates' property. The poor thing had tangled with a porcupine. She took him to the vet and paid for his treatment."

Melanie chuckled.

"She's a colleague. Nothing more."

"Oh, brother dear. Your tone of voice says different."

"It's stopped raining. Can we go riding after lunch?" Haley asked.

Saved by the question, Flynn wiped his mouth and avoided Melanie's skeptical expression. "I'd like to ride with you girls, but I haven't been on a regular bike in ages."

"You can use Mother's. She doesn't ride much." Sitting beside him, Pam grabbed his arm. "Please, Uncle Flynn."

"You'd better take my bike." Stan folded his napkin. "Otherwise, I'll have to raise the saddle and handlebars on Melanie's."

"But that means you won't ride with us. Remember, I can't ride for very long." How could he be sure his nieces would be safe on the trail?

Stan scooted back from the table and poked his head out the French doors. "Looks like it will rain again soon so you all need to stay in the cul-de-sac."

"Okaaay." Haley rolled her eyes.

"Help clear the table, girls, then you can go riding." Melanie sighed and poked Flynn's arm. "Go have fun with your nieces since I won't get any more details about Jo from you."

Once dishes were in the dishwasher, Stan opened the garage while the girls donned their helmets and straddled their bikes.

Flynn strapped on Stan's helmet, swung his good leg over the crossbar, and set his foot on the pedal. He had not taken his new brace—which arrived late Friday—into consideration and hesitated a second before pushing off. Good thing the driveway slanted toward the road. He wobbled trying to gain his balance, which proved difficult since his left foot didn't flex when he pedaled. But after a couple of near-collisions with the curb, he managed to stay upright and maintained a reasonable speed. At least he kept pace with Pam.

Stan and Melanie watched for vehicles, and the three riders circled the cul-de-sac and back to the house several times before Flynn had to call it quits.

"Sorry, kids. I can't keep up with you."

Haley stopped beside him. "Is your leg hurting?"

"Just a bit, sweet child."

Heavy raindrops splattered the driveway. Stan called, "Come inside, girls."

Shaking off moisture, they all entered the house through the kitchen door. Melanie served blackberry pie and ice-cream, and ten minutes later, Haley and Pam ran upstairs, leaving the adults in the living room.

Flynn took the opportunity to tell Stan and Melanie about his plans for the motel. "Jo checked the zoning restrictions for that area, and if I can purchase the building, I will be allowed to use the rooms for veterans."

"I know the homeless vet problem has been on your heart for a while. I'm proud of you, brother. How can we help?" Melanie wiped at a tear on her cheek.

"I'm seeking funds from a variety of sources."

"Say no more." Rocking in his chair, Stan added, "We'll donate to the cause."

"Thanks." Flynn kept his big question until almost time to leave. "Um, have you heard from Ian? How is he?"

"He texts occasionally. Never was one for frequent communication. He's overseas right now, and said he'd come visit when he gets back." Melanie hiked a shoulder. "I suppose he still doesn't talk to you."

The familiar knot formed in Flynn's chest. "Right. But let me know when he's scheduled to visit you and I'll make a point of coming over. He won't make a scene in front of his nieces."

"I'll keep you informed. Any other news you want to share?"

How did Melanie always know when he had something on his mind? But he'd already decided he wouldn't tell anyone about Geena's message. The fewer people who knew about her, the better.

"Nope." He eased out of the armchair. "I need to head to the ferry. Thanks for a great meal and good company." He rubbed the tight muscles in his thigh.

"And a bike ride I won't forget in a hurry."

Melanie hugged him and whispered, "Don't forget Haley wants cousins."

He climbed into his truck before she could see the blush creeping up his neck.

Later, while on the ferry, his phone dinged indicating a text. From Jo.

> *The dog is okay. He was micro-chipped, and the veterinarian located his ecstatic owner. Hope you enjoyed the day with your sister and family.*

He scowled at the driver in the vehicle beside him, then stared at his phone. *And how was your day, Jo? Who rode with you? Was it a guy?*

No way would he ask her such questions, but he'd give anything to find out. Not because he was jealous. Nope. Because he needed to protect Jo from another bad choice in companions.

Chapter 12

Bikes secured, storage unit locked, Jo drove home, the endorphins still circulating through her body. Gerry had a great sense of humor and the ride with him had been fun. He seemed content in her company, and although still wary of men in general, she had to admit she'd enjoyed the day with him. He'd also gained a couple of points by expressing concern and sympathy when the veterinary clinic called to report on the dog. All was well, and the owner had been located.

Ready for a shower, she entered her bedroom and screeched to a halt. The sliding door to her closet was open and all her shoe boxes were strewn across the carpet. Shoes, boots, littered the carpet. The hairs on the back of her neck prickled. She glanced around the room. Nothing else seemed out of place. Even the limited contents of her jewelry box on the dresser were all present. Not that she had anything of value anyway.

She retraced her steps down the hall. The closet door was open an inch. She never left it that way. The contents on the top shelf had been moved, the hangers shifted to the side, but otherwise, all as she remembered. In the living room, she did a quick inventory. Again, nothing appeared to be missing. Her laptop, the most important item of any value, was still in her briefcase beside the sofa. As she stood in the middle of the room, the sheer curtain over the patio door quivered ever so slightly. She pushed it aside and discovered the door open a fraction, enough to allow the cool breeze to slither through. The point of entry as she hadn't been on the patio in ages.

Before she called the police, she returned to the chaos in her bedroom. Whatever the intruder come for must have been in there. Someone with a shoe fetish? Except none of her footwear was missing. She sat on the carpet about to return shoes to boxes, but halted. If she contacted the authorities, she needed to leave the scene as she found it. She hiked a shoulder. Since nothing had been taken, was it worth wasting their time? For sure, she'd ask Flynn what home security system he used and install a similar model. And place a stout stick along the track to prevent the patio door from being opened from the outside.

As she sat amidst the mess, she had a lightbulb moment. Shoeboxes. Only her shoeboxes had been messed with. She'd found a shoebox at Nelda's house. Filled with little toys. Was there a connection? She scrambled over to the bed and patted under it until she located the plastic bag. On her knees, she dumped the contents on her bed and riffled through the items.

Characters from children's movies or cartoons. A few cars. A small doll. Nothing special. The last object she picked up resembled a chess piece, a castle. Odd one out. She twisted the top and it popped off, revealing a flash drive.

The enormity of the discovery hit Jo like a punch to the chest. She sucked in a breath and stood. The intruder must be Rosie or Wade, or someone connected to the illegal activities conducted on Nelda's property. Thumb drive tucked into her pocket, she nabbed her phone, and called Deputy Frances Gordon.

Seated on the sofa, Jo described the situation, eyes on the now closed patio door.

"We'll be there in ten minutes." The deputy's voice held a note of excitement.

Jo folded her arms as the muscles in her gut coiled. If only she could call someone to console her. Dad would come, but then Mother would insist she move back home. Gerry? No. Jo didn't want to invite him into her home. And Flynn? Still in Seattle, no doubt.

A knock on the door put the brakes on her self-pity. Jo spied two deputies through the peep hole and invited them in.

Gordon opened a plastic evidence bag. "Place the thumb drive in here, please."

Jo complied. "Do you want all the other toys, too? They're on my bed."

"I'll get them." Deputy Zach Davis headed down the hall.

While he was gone, Gordon pointed to the patio door. "You touched the handle?"

"I had to close it. Sorry. I wasn't—"

"Don't worry. We may still be able to lift fingerprints, especially from the outside." The deputy sealed the evidence bag. "I brought a fingerprint kit with me."

The investigative process took the rest of the afternoon. As the deputies were about to leave, Gordon said, "By the way, our tech department reported the email account for Charles Freeman was disabled the day you discovered the ammunition containers. Which adds to our case. We haven't been able to locate Rosie or Wade, either. Of course, we lifted many prints from Mrs. Yate's home and the ammunition containers. Maybe these prints will point to the renters or someone else in their organization."

"Thanks for the update." The deputies left and Jo locked the door. For extra protection, she moved a heavy side table in front of it and broke a broom handle in two and wedged one piece in the patio door track.

After a quick shower, she raided the refrigerator and only found ingredients for an omelet. A trip to the grocery store loomed in her future. With little time to prepare fancy dishes, her culinary needs were easily met. Flipping the omelet onto her plate, she wondered if Flynn's sister had sent leftovers home with him. Or if he decided to spend the night.

Nothing held Jo's attention during the evening. No

TV show nor mystery novel. Not even sending time with her cycling buddies. She lay awake under the covers, ears attuned for the slightest unusual sound. Her thoughts veered from Wade and Rosie to Flynn. And his comment about why he kept a Bible in his truck. *For people like you.*

He'd offered to guide her back to the Savior. Yeah. She'd deserted God, and if Flynn asked why, she wasn't sure she could explain her actions. Granted, Phil's duplicity had shattered her self-confidence, and later, when she developed complications during her pregnancy, she'd prayed for the baby's health, but she miscarried anyway. Jo had always taken that as a punishment for her indiscretions. Deep down, she knew her reasoning didn't gel with what she remembered from Bible studies in her youth. God was not like Zeus on Mount Olympus hurling lightning bolts at sinners. But if Mother knew about the miscarriage, she'd probably agree with Jo's original false assumption.

Gritting her teeth, she threw off the covers and paced her bedroom. Mother. Again, a sliver of a memory lurked in the darkest corners of Jo's heart. She acknowledged these glimpses into her blocked recollections had been triggered by Phil's reentry into her life, but why would that event expose a memory concerning Mother?

Certain she wouldn't be able to sleep, Jo brewed a mug of coffee, sat on the sofa, and covered herself with a light blanket. She leaned back and closed her eyes. If ever she was to have peace of mind again, she had to penetrate her amnesia barricade. She reviewed the wedding plans in minute detail. The actual ceremony. Yeah, she recalled every incident as if it happened last week.

Revisiting the months that followed were as painful as deliberately hitting her thumb with a hammer. Over and over. Only Kendy and Serena knew about her pregnancy, accompanying her when she registered at a neighborhood clinic. Jo had dropped out of university, giving up her track-and-field scholarship, and moved to a studio apartment south of Seattle. Although Kendy offered her money, she took a job in a convenience store. Jo refused to visit her folks, not even her father.

Eyes open, Jo sucked in deep breaths. So far, so good. Nothing unusual, no gaps exposed yet. Her day-to-day activities had been limited by lack of funds and painful cramps. She sipped the last of her coffee and hurried through the next months of memories, and although they cut through her mind as efficiently as hot steel through ice, there were no surprises. The amnesia must be hiding later events. After the miscarriage.

Mentally taxed, Jo needed a break and made another mug of coffee. Seated again, she set the mug on the side table and glanced at a photograph. Kendy as a high school cheerleader. Shoulder-length brunette tresses, eyes bright with excitement, her cleft chin—always a trait remarked upon. Jo jerked as if one of Zeus's bolts jabbed her heart. The beautiful face of her sister pried open the barrier, revealing snippets of events Jo hadn't recalled in nearly eight years. Way back then, she'd met someone who looked remarkably like Kendy.

Jo's heart thrashed about as if it were a fish in a dry bucket, but she had to delve into the abyss. A sip of coffee, warm mug held with both hands, she forged ahead.

Following the miscarriage, she had attended a support group for women and couples who'd suffered the loss of a baby, either before or after birth. The counseling did help her realize her life was not over and she could still have a productive future.

Another zap to her heart. The face of Robert, the counselor, loomed large in front of Jo. He had thick, dark hair, deep chocolate eyes framed by the longest lashes she'd ever seen on a man. And a cleft chin.

Jo straightened as a conversation repeated in her mind. Robert admitted his girlfriend had a miscarriage. "She couldn't face me, and after she gave me the sad news, she left Seattle."

The rest of that meeting blurred in and out of focus. Did Jo speak to the man? Did Robert provide any other details about his girlfriend? Jo forced her resurfacing memories to slow-motion mode. What happened after he made the declaration?

Another attendee asked if he'd ever seen his girlfriend again. "No, she moved to Gig Harbor."

"Did you try to keep in touch?"

"I did. I wanted to make sure my Annie was okay."

A tearful woman asked, "What happened to her?"

"She married a guy in the US Marines."

Jo dropped her mug, and it smashed on the floor. She'd never reviewed this conversation since it occurred. No wonder she'd suppressed the memory in an amnesia vault. Robert's girlfriend was her mother. And she hadn't had a miscarriage—she'd married Dad and Kendall was born less than nine months later.

Kendy had inherited her father's brunette locks, chocolate-colored eyes surrounded by long lashes, and his cleft chin. Jo threw aside the blanket, stepped around the mess on the floor, and strode to the bookshelf where she displayed photographs. She examined a family portrait closely. Anyone could tell Dad was Jo's father. But Kendy looked nothing like either parent. Why hadn't Jo noticed before?

And mother? The smug expression on her face in her wedding picture soured Jo's stomach. What a fraud. Hypocrite. Always nagging her girls *to keep themselves for marriage*. Did Dad know? How about Kendy?

The more Jo dwelt on the truth, the more she seethed. Was this the reason she never returned to worship services? Had she allowed what she knew about her mother to come between her and God? That was giving Mother way too much power.

Jo paced again. She had to discuss her discovery with someone. Certainly not her sister, and although her biking buddies were good friends, she had no desire to share her dilemma with Emma, Vic, or Danny. The only other person she could think of was Flynn. But not at three o'clock in the morning. He attended Hillside Bible Fellowship in Silverdale. She'd visit with him tomorrow.

In a daze, Jo cleaned up the coffee and shattered mug. She moved as slowly as an aged sloth. Her muscles appeared to be losing strength minute by minute. She collapsed onto the sofa, covered herself, and closed her eyes. Her exhaled breath seemed to go on forever as if her mind, body, and soul were deflating like a punctured pool float. She fell into a deep sleep and only awoke close to nine when upstairs neighbors dropped a heavy object in their living room.

Still determined to speak to Flynn, Jo searched online for the address of the church and the worship times. As she applied her makeup, she noticed her face had lost its hard edges. She couldn't pinpoint exactly what had happened at first, but then she realized she no longer clenched her jaw, and her smile reached her eyes. Why? Because she'd gained back *all* her memories, even the traumatic ones, or because she now had no reason to keep rejecting God? Or both?

She deliberately arrived late and sat at the back of the small meeting hall. Halfway through the service, Flynn walked to the front and led a prayer. He concentrated on giving thanks for their blessings, especially the freedom with which they could gather and worship. A lump formed in Jo's throat. She had taken that privilege for granted and had neglected God for too long.

Ready to absorb more reminders of her Christian teachings, she looked up in time to see Flynn return to his seat next to a blonde wearing a red top. Who looked a lot like Serena from the back. Unable to focus on the rest of the service, Jo hurried out and sat in her vehicle, breathing hard and clenching her fists.

Chapter 13

Reverting back to old habits came too easily. Jo relaxed and disposed of the negative descriptors for Serena she'd accumulated in her mind. She'd spent hours the previous night discovering how her reaction to her mother's past had curdled her relationship with God, and she wasn't about to let her hostile feelings toward Serena crush the fragile faith to which she clung. However, she did hope her former friend and Flynn wouldn't leave together.

As the congregants exited the building, the blonde wearing a red top walked right past Jo's SUV. Not Serena. She grinned and watched for Flynn. A few minutes later, he came out accompanied by a couple of young men. They chatted briefly, then Flynn headed toward his truck.

Jo slid from her vehicle and waved to him.

He returned the gesture and approached her. "Hey. This is a surprise. Did you attend the service?"

She hesitated, then told him the truth. "I stayed for a short time, but, um, I thought I saw Serena and the old animosity stirred in my heart. I had to leave." She leaned against her vehicle and huffed out a breath. "I really need to talk to you. Do you have lunch plans?"

"None that can't be changed."

"Good. Will you join me?"

They arranged to meet in the parking lot of a seafood restaurant overlooking the water. Jo opened her door and added, "Please bring your Bible."

His eyes lit up and he smiled broadly. "I will."

Once inside the restaurant, Jo asked for a secluded table and ignored the waiter's raised eyebrows. After they ordered, she set her elbows on the table. "If you don't mind, I'd like to eat first then discuss my problem. I had a rough night and I'm starving."

"Fine by me."

Surrounded by enticing aromas of her broiled shrimp and Flynn's seafood platter, and the buzz of patrons' chatter and clinking cutlery, Jo appreciated him for honoring her request. He described his day with his family and didn't ask her any questions while they completed their meal.

He rubbed his thigh. "My leg muscles are still complaining."

"That sounds like fun." She recalled a previous conversation. "But not a tandem, right?"

"Right." He harrumphed. "How was your ride yesterday?"

"I don't want to discuss it." She lowered her head and pushed aside her plate. Gerry had no part in her present predicament. And for some reason, Jo didn't want Flynn to know about him.

"Why? Who were you with?" He leaned forward. "What did he do? Did he hurt you?"

"What a ridiculous question. Of course, he didn't." Rolling her eyes, she wiped her mouth and crumpled the paper napkin. "I need your help with my spiritual life. Not my love life. Which is none of your business."

"Sorry. I got carried away. I just want to make sure you're…safe."

"Ha. Safe. I could have used your concern yesterday." She described the events that colored her afternoon and evening.

"Has the deputy told you what's on the flash drive?"

She shook her head.

"Why didn't you call me? I would have gone right over." His gray eyes narrowed, and his brow furrowed. "After lunch, I'm going to install a security system at your apartment. Even if it's just an over-the-counter model. Until we order a more sophisticated type, I can spend the night on your sofa."

"I agree to the security system, but not you spending the night. I can take care of myself. You're not my bodyguard."

"Do you know any self-defense moves? You can attend my classes."

She shook her head.

"It's…I care about you." He ran a finger around his

collar and Jo was sure his neck reddened. "You, and all my agents."

Shrugging, she tilted her head. "Thank you, but can we get back to the reason I need your advice?" She'd deal with his overbearing attitude and apparent embarrassment later.

He huffed out a sigh. "Okay. I'm ready to listen."

The waiter removed their plates and refilled glasses of tea.

Jo cleared her throat then described in detail what she experienced when she couldn't sleep. Flynn let her talk uninterruptedly. By the time she completed the revelation exposed when she shattered the amnesia wall, her tea glass was empty but her heart was full, ready to bust wide open. She folded her arms to curtail the explosion. "You can see why I need help. On the one hand I'm thankful I have my memories back, but now what should I do with this knowledge? I know there are Scriptures that deal with a hypocrite."

"You're correct. Let me—"

"If we read them, will they tell me how to handle Mother's hypocrisy?" On the verge of teas, Jo blinked and took in a shuddering breath. "All during our teenage years, she'd make Kendy and me listen to her spiel about dating, about the seriousness of choosing the right spouse, and against getting pregnant before marriage. How do I reconcile Mother's behavior with a desire to return to the Shepherd, as you once stated?" She leaned back and lifted her gaze to Flynn's face.

Brows knitted and mouth in a soft curve, he lowered his chin and took her hand. "Oh, my dear Jo. I knew something traumatic happened to you in the past to damage your relationship with God, but I had no idea how deeply you were hurt. By Phil, the miscarriage, and what you learned about your mom. How can I help you?"

She lifted her other hand to the table and he held it as well. The warmth from his touch reached her heart. "I don't know exactly. Talking about the events has eased the tension in my core, but I have to deal with Mother's behavior. You know, being a hypocrite. There's a Scripture about taking the plank out of your eye before you criticize the person who has a speck of sawdust in her eye."

Flynn released her hands and opened his Bible. "Right. Matthew 7:3–5. But those verses can also refer to someone who expects forgiveness but doesn't give it. Let's slow down a bit."

Jo swallowed against the lump in her throat. "Okay, so I'm no expert."

"Before I refer to other Scriptures, we must prioritize your needs. First of all, and I'm going to be blunt, did your miscarriage turn you away from God?"

Jo had deliberated the idea before. "No. I had a rough pregnancy, and by the time I lost the baby, I'd already stopped attending worship services and my prayer life was negligible."

"Why?"

"I was wallowing in self-pity. I don't remember blaming God because I viewed the event as a deserved punishment."

Flynn gasped and she held up her hand to ward off his response. "I know my reasoning was flawed. I think the final separation happened after Robert told the group about his girlfriend's miscarriage, and I made the connection to Mother and Kendy." Jo wrapped her arms around her middle this time. Tangled knots in her gut fought with her recent meal. "I...I need water, please."

He motioned to the waiter who delivered two glasses of water. "Thanks. I know we're hogging your table, but I'll leave a worthwhile tip."

The young man loped away.

Jo sipped the cold liquid and her lunch settled. "When I reflected on Kendy and my dad and wondered if they knew about Mother's past, that's what turned me off religion in general. Mother's hypocritical behavior and her attitude toward me. At the time, I thought she favored Kendall because of Robert. Maybe she loved him more that Dad."

"Whoa, Jo. You're making a lot of assumptions."

"I know. But that's what I felt back then. And probably why I locked away the events."

"Does your mother know about your miscarriage? Maybe it reminded her—"

"No. Only Kendy and Serena knew. Yes, Serena. She was my college roommate and bridesmaid."

"Why the animosity now?"

Wiping the condensation off the glass, Jo hiked a shoulder. "Her attitude toward me changed when I started working for my folks."

"She's jealous of you."

Jo reared back and laughed. "Jealous? Of what?"

Flynn took her hands again. "Your relationship with your parents."

Not wanting to be distracted by his touch, she pulled away and picked up her glass. "I don't understand."

"How long has Serena been in real estate?"

"Since she graduated. Worked for a couple of small companies at first, then joined Tremaine Realty."

"In other words, she's dedicated to the business, spent years in the field, and along you come, what a year ago? Your parents hire you and already your sales rival hers. I checked when I signed on."

"You have a point." Jo sipped her water.

"And her threat to tell your folks about the miscarriage is her way of controlling you."

"You're right. She doesn't think I should be successful in her area of expertise and probably wants me out."

"I surprised Serena hasn't disclosed your miscarriage already. She could have severely damaged your relationship with your mother."

Jo blew out a breath. "That relationship might be shattered soon. I have to ask Mother about Kendall's parentage."

"Agreed. But speak to her in private. Let her be the one to tell your father and sister, if she hasn't already."

Nodding, Jo shifted in her seat. She had an idea what he would say next.

"And you must tell her about your miscarriage."

"I know. I know." She stifled a chuckle. "It'll be easier now that I no longer work in the Gig Harbor office. I won't have to face her disapproving looks every day."

"She might surprise you."

"I doubt it. Whenever I date a guy, she always pushes for marriage and more grandchildren. Take my last boyfriend, Max Hadfield. We broke up during my recent vacation. When I told Mother, she reacted as if I'd killed the man. She agreed with him that I should give up my career and the bike club." Jo muttered under her breath, "Domineering jerk."

But Flynn heard. "Ahh, no wonder you objected to my earlier interference in your life. Sorry. I won't infringe on your independence." Flynn drained his glass. "But I will keep an eye out for your safety. Okay?"

She picked up her paper napkin and gave him a brief smile.

The waiter came by and offered to refill their glasses. Flynn declined, as did Jo. She folded the napkin, smoothed out the wrinkles. Time to leave? She reached for her purse slung over the back of her chair.

He tapped the table. "Please stay a little longer. I

know you've bared your soul, and I'm honored to be the person you chose, but I'd like to go back to the miscarriage, if that's all right."

"I suppose."

"You probably discussed all this with the support group back then, but how did you feel?"

She'd relived those months last night, and sharing her state of mind and heart again were like removing the stitches from a wound and peeling back the skin. She frowned and intertwined her fingers in her lap.

"I'm sure it'll be hard, but I think—and I'm no counselor—you need to confront those emotions before you talk to your mother. Although you found out about her relationship with Robert at that time, she was not to blame for your miscarriage."

Flynn's reason made sense. She had to remove her personal experience from the equation and sucked in a deep breath. "As you can image, I was devastated. I was two-and-a-half months along and had finally come to terms with being a single mother. Kendy had kept in touch and actually came to the hospital when I hemorrhaged. Doctor said the fetus wasn't viable." Jo lowered her head. Waves of sadness threatened to down her. She gulped, panted.

"Please continue. You're safe and I won't let anything happen to you." The concern in his voice rescued her.

She raised her head. "I didn't handle the loss well. Became depressed, considered ending it all, but then joined the support group which helped me connect with other women who had similar experiences. I eventually returned to university, opened my business, but obtained my real estate license just in case." She scoffed and withdrew her hands. "Never in my wildest dreams did I think I'd need my backup plan."

"I'm glad you're working for your parents. Otherwise, I wouldn't have met you."

Again, his words and tone penetrated her numb mind and heart. "I'm thankful they employed me, too." She wasn't about to add meeting him had given a glimmer of hope to her life.

"Next question." Flynn folded his arms. "I'm asking because I think it's important for you to face, if you haven't already. Has your miscarriage affected how you feel about having children in the future?"

Eyebrows raised, Jo leaned back and stared at Flynn. She had given the topic consideration in the past, but she agreed, she had to address the matter. "I did wonder what kind of mother I would have been. Cold and critical like my mom, or loving and supportive like Kendy? And as to kids in my future—maybe." She shook her head and chuckled. "But first I have to find the right guy, preferably one who isn't still married or a control freak." There. She'd laid her cards down, face up. "What about you? Kids to join your nieces?" The question spilled out before she could reign in her tongue. But he'd introduced the subject.

His turn to chuckle. "Haley asked me last week

about having children because she needs cousins. But children to me mean a happy marriage, and I don't deserve one."

"Whoa Mr. McCaul. What do you mean?"

"It's my fault Mom and Dad died. I deprived Melanie and Ian of parents, Haley and Pam of grandparents. And countless people of strong, Christian friends."

"Why does that equate to you not getting married? You were engaged to Geena."

He narrowed his eyes at her, a hint of doubt clouding his expression. "Our relationship began before the accident. During rehab, I had a notion to break off the engagement, but she beat me to it. And I was relieved."

"Relived because you believed you didn't deserve a happy life, or because you didn't love her any longer?" *Jo, what are you doing? Why do you want to know?* In an effort to hide her embarrassment and confusion, she set the salt and pepper shakers side-by-side, straightened the sweetener and sugar packets in the little holder.

"Hey, how did this conversation suddenly focus on my love life?"

"As opposed to my *whole* life?"

"Touché. But forget about me and let's address one more important topic."

"Okay, but the waiter is getting antsy."

"I know. This part won't take long." Flynn placed a

hand on top of his Bible. "Are you serious about returning to the Shepherd?"

Was she ready to recommit herself? Jo picked up the napkin again, tore pieces off and mounded them together. Her life resembled the pile of scraps, and she was tired of feeling broken. She gazed at Flynn, admiring the serenity that seemed to emanate from his face. "I am."

He smiled and leaned forward once more. "Great. First, let me remind you that we have all sinned and fallen short."

"I remember that verse."

"Romans 3:21. Once you set your mind in gear, more Scriptures will come back to you. I'm proud to be a Christian, but I'm human, a work in progress, so don't expect perfection from me. However, I'm honored you asked for my help. Be prepared for a few hard truths. Instead of reading a slew of Scriptures, I'll paraphrase, and then give you the list so you can review them at home. You do have a Bible, right?"

"Packed away in my storage unit. I'll search for it after we leave here."

"Good. And I'll purchase a security system and install it today."

She appreciated his desire to keep her safe now. "How do I fix my relationship with God?"

"When you were baptized, you entered into a covenant with God. Due to life events, you drifted away. All you need to do is repent, ask for forgiveness, establish a prayer-life, and live as a follower of Christ." He turned toward the back of his Bible. "John reminds us to confess our sins and God will forgive us. I John 1:9."

Eyes closed, Jo allowed Flynn's words to penetrate her soul. God would forgive her, but what about her need to forgive her mom? She opened her eyes and set her elbows on the table again. "I know I must deal with Mother. That's going to be hard."

"Maybe one of the toughest things you've ever done, but necessary to heal the wounds. You must concentrate on the health of your soul by overcoming the hurdles in your life. I think forgiveness might be your greatest challenge." He flipped to another Scripture. "Paul tells us in Ephesians 4:32 to forgive each other as Christ has forgiven us."

By now the lunch crowd had thinned, and Jo glanced at the empty tables. The waiter hovered and casually placed the bill on the table. She instantly set her hand over it.

Flynn closed his Bible and raised his eyebrows at her.

"My treat. Please. I know we need to leave, but I have one more person to address. Serena." Jo's heart fluttered, but not in a positive way. "She contacted Phil and told him I wanted to see him. Which isn't true. He's emailed me a few times."

"Instead of viewing her action as a problem, you could thank her."

"What?"

"Didn't you say recalling your time with Phil, and your miscarriage helped open your memory vault?"

"Yeah. But be thankful for Serena?"

"Just because we forgive a person doesn't mean we are required to become best pals."

Jo could find no fault in anything Flynn said, no matter how hard to hear. His advice and reminders from Scripture were exactly what she needed. "Thank you. I'm ready to go. How about you?"

He stood and drew out his wallet. "I'm leaving the tip, remember."

They exited the restaurant and he walked with her to her vehicle. Fluffy, white clouds glided across the blue sky and birds sang in the rhododendron bushes lining the parking lot. What a perfect day.

Jo hadn't felt so alive in years. She popped the remote, but didn't open her door. A nagging thought pecked at her sense of wellbeing. Leaning against the SUV, she shoved her hands into her pockets. "I, um, need to add something else about Mother." Head lowered, she said, "Mother has many positive qualities. She's thoughtful, kind. I remember one Christmas back when Dad was stationed at the Miramar Marine Corps Air Station near San Diego. A young Marine and his family stayed with us for a week or so because their apartment burned down. Anyway, Mother bought the kids presents and placed them under our tree." Jo nudged a small stick with her booted toe. "I've never forgotten the looks on the children's faces. Probably five and six years old."

Before she could react, Flynn drew her into a hug. "I haven't met Kendall yet, but I know Anita and Thomas did a wonderful job raising you. Hardworking. Generous, kind. Those traits didn't just fall out of the sky."

Head on his shoulder, Jo slid her arms around his waist and inhaled his subtle scent which reminded her of cedar. Yup. He could keep her safe any time he wanted.

Chapter 14

Forcing the memory of Jo in his arms from his mind, Flynn unlocked the office door in Silverdale and slumped in his desk chair. Other than to offer comfort, he had no business hugging her. Afterall, he didn't deserve happiness. He accepted his rationalization and opened the drawer to his right. Late Friday, he'd tossed a slip of paper in there and now needed the details from the message. He located the note and entered the contact information of the organization into his phone, which he should have done when the client provided the name of a man who often contributed to projects for veterans.

Task complete, Flynn noted the Bible on his desk. He'd used the copy from his pickup for the meeting with Jo. Their lunchtime conversation paraded through his mind. She had endured much in her early twenties, but in spite of her setbacks, she was a strong woman and he was certain she could forge a fruitful life for herself, free from pressures that ate away at her self-confidence.

He doodled on a notepad as he reflected on her cold attitude toward him later that afternoon while he installed her security system. She'd barely spoken to him and avoided eye contact. He couldn't decide if she regretted his outline for returning to God, or the hug. At the time, she sank against his chest and didn't push away, but later, he was certain she wanted him out of her apartment as quickly as possible.

Flynn closed his eyes. "Father God, please be with Jo and help her to forgive and move on. Thank You for Your grace." He paused, frowned as a sharp pain stabbed his soul. What? Without understanding why, he added, "Please, also be with Ian and keep him safe."

Eyes wide, he picked up the Bible and fanned through the pages until he found the letter. From Ian. The last correspondence in any form he'd received from his brother. Although Flynn knew the contents by heart, he read the words again.

> *Why didn't you follow my advice and drive to Cle Elum and buy a new valve*
> *for the stove? It's your fault our parents are dead. And I'm glad your scars*
> *will be constant reminders of your arrogance.*

Flynn threw the letter across the office. "Yes, Ian, I admit the accident was my fault. I've apologized to you and Melanie so many times. She forgave me. Why can't you?" He shoved back his chair, strode to the reception area, and stared out the window. Not many cars in the lot today. To quell the rising panic, he counted the trees. Numerous trees. A few minutes later, his pulse dropping to an acceptable level, he returned to his desk and opened his Bible. He flipped to the book of Matthew chapter seven and scanned the first four verses. Then he focused on verse five, the hypocrisy admonition Jo referenced. He read it aloud. "You hypocrite, first take the plank out of your own eye, and then you will see clearly to remove the speck from your brother's eye."

The reality hit him like a sledgehammer to the gut. The Scripture used the word "brother" which in the context of the chapter included non-relatives, but Flynn took it literally. The situation did apply to him and his brother. He wanted so much to reconnect with Ian and had accused him of not wanting to meet. But maybe his brother saw the plank in Flynn's eye and resented his insistence they reconcile without acknowledging his own faults.

Leaning back, Flynn recalled the day they arrived at the cabin, the day before the explosion, but this time he paid close attention to his attitude and his brother's words. "Check with Stan. Drive into Cle Elum. Buy a replacement part."

His exact response to Ian. "We'll only be here for three days. Everyone who uses the stove knows to light the burners as soon as they are turned on. I've cautioned the kids. Who are you to question my reasoning? I don't want to drive anywhere. Go play with your nieces."

What arrogance. As the owner of a construction company, Stan would have been the perfect person to inspect the stove. But did Flynn ask him? Noooo.

Flynn rammed his chair back with such force it bounced off the wall. Why had he never recalled his word before? He couldn't blame the omission on anything comparable to Jo's amnesia. Must be his conceit, haughtiness that concealed his behavior. No wonder Ian wanted nothing to do with him. Flynn rubbed his thigh. Seems whenever his heart ached, so did his leg.

Did Melanie know the reason Ian refused contact? Flynn took a chance and called her. He described his remembered encounter and asked, "Did Ian confide in you?"

"He did, but he asked me not to tell you. You insulted him, belittled him. No wonder he hasn't contacted you. But I suggest you apologize, and then maybe he'll agree to talk."

"I will. Oh, my dear God. All these years he's believed I have such a low opinion of him. No wonder he ignores me. Please ask him to read my email. Thanks, sis."

Flynn returned to his desk and opened his laptop. Whenever he phoned or texted, Ian declined the call or didn't respond. It took thirty minutes to compose an apology message. Before Flynn hit *send*, he prayed. "Please dear Father, soften Ian's heart so he'll open my email and contact me. Forgive me for my pride and attitude of superiority and replace it with humbleness."

Knowing Ian was out of the country didn't prevent Flynn from checking his email every couple of minutes. While he waited, he reviewed plans from Landon Hunt, scheduled to begin work on Nelda's house the next day. An hour later, Flynn was ready to close his account when a new message popped up. From Wesley, not Ian. Huffing out a big sigh, he opened the email.

> *Thanks for agreeing to my move. I'm working with two clients who want to purchase homes in the Tacoma area. Iris's pain has eased. Probably because she's no longer stressed about Noah. Speaking of him, he's settling well into his group home. He's even made some friends, one has a connection to you.*

Flynn frowned and continued reading.

> *I met Lewis Pierce while packing my vehicle when I left the Silverdale office.*
>
> *He said you had dated his sister.*

Rocking in his chair, Flynn nodded. Yeah. He remembered Jo had mentioned seeing them chat.

> *Well, Lewis was at Noah's home yesterday. He explained he has a stepson who*

*also has William's syndrome. We're going
to encourage our sons' friendship.*

*What a coincidence. Give my best to all at the
office.*

Muscles in Flynn's gut churned. Coincidence?
Maybe.

If only he had a way to contact Geena. She'd know
whether or not Lewis had a stepson.

Chapter 15

The following week sped by as if propelled by a jet engine. Jo had spent most of the time working alongside Flynn on Nelda's house. She'd been embarrassed at first, recalling her confession, his compassion, the hug, and then she gave him the cold shoulder when he installed her security system.

Not once did he refer back to their meeting. In fact, he seemed more relaxed and less…domineering. He joked with her and the other workers, and she admired how he didn't expect them to do anything he wasn't prepared to do himself. The fact he spoke fluent Spanish aided his ability to communicate specific instructions. Flynn proved to be skilled in many areas. No wonder he had calloused hands.

He'd left early on Tuesday to hold the first session of self-defense classes. Wednesday morning, he reported he only had two students, but wasn't discouraged. He did invite Jo again, but she'd refused with the assurance she'd consider in the future. Instead of being irritated by his insistence, she considered it a positive—he did care about her safety. However, that evening at the gym, she had spent extra time with the arm weights. If anyone attacked her, she had to increase her upper body strength.

On Friday, Jo stepped into the long hall from Nelda's master bedroom, approached the grand staircase, and held onto the carved oak banister. Recalling her Sunday conversation with Flynn had reminded her of major items on her to-do list and she needed to be on her own. She hadn't yet confronted…no, spoken to Mother. She'd tried to phone several times, but chickened out at the last minute. Yesterday, Mom called, and Jo prepared to ask for a meeting, but Mother's end of the conversation was short and specific. "Joanna dear, will you be bringing a plus-one to my party? Remember my old friend Cheryl? Well, her son is recently divorced and—"

"I will." Not again. Mother's next attempt to set her up with some eligible guy. "I hope to bring…Gerry."

"Oh, a new boyfriend? I can't wait to meet him. I'll let Cheryl know. See you Saturday. And Joanna, please wear something feminine."

Jo had immediately called Gerry and apologized for the short notice. He seemed overjoyed to be invited and agreed only if she'd join him for a picnic the following Saturday. Jo had already found out Flynn's sister would be in town, and he'd invited her. Not only would Gerry as an escort pacify Mother, but Jo could pretend, and maybe convince herself, she wasn't interested in Flynn romantically. The way she'd nestled against his shoulder after their meeting last Sunday had been a one-off.

But she wasn't blind. Flynn did get his hands dirty and seemed to enjoy the role of builder more than that of a realtor. Besides, he usually wore old jeans and T-shirts that were a size or two too small. Jo wiped sweat off her upper lip. She had to quit ogling and find something to do while waiting for the landscaper Jackson Reed's visit. Flynn was a colleague, and other than listening to her and treating her with respect, he'd shown no signs of romance.

Descending the stairs, Jo noted the spindles had been replaced. A perfect job. She couldn't tell where the broken ones had been. She was impressed with the crew from Strategic Repairs. Landon Hunt earned his title as supervisor. The work done so far had been completed on time and to a high standard.

Jackson Reed was scheduled to arrive in fifteen minutes. Enough time for a trip down to the bay. Jo sat on the dock and after removing her boots and socks, dangled her toes in the cold water that splashed gently against the pier. Other than the closing on the Underwoods' sale, she had no pressing work and took the respite to focus again on changes she was applying to her life.

Flynn's advice was easy to listen to, but hard to implement. Pray. Forgive. Ask God for forgiveness. She'd done the third step, trusting in God's grace, but struggled with one and two. Especially two. In order to forgive Mother, Jo would have to dig deep into her fledgling relationship with God and pray for strength. And somewhere along the way, she'd have to face Serena and Phil.

She used her socks to dry her feet, then slipped on her boots. Pray? *Yes, Jo, you can.* The best guidance she'd ever received about praying came from a Youth Minister at their church when Jo was thirteen, fourteen. He'd told the group of young teens to talk to God as if He were their earthly father, grandfather, or trusted friend. "Pour out your heart. Say thank you. Ask for help for yourself or for friends. Don't be shy. Your Heavenly Father loves you and wants the best for you." So different to the staid, rote phrases Jo had often heard in worship services.

"Please, God, help me talk to Mother without animosity or judgement." A brisk wind blew over Jo and small waves formed in the water. A nearby potted Alpine mint bush released its soothing scent. She inhaled, stood, and gazed over the bay. God moved in mysterious ways. Calmness wrapped its arms around her, and she sighed. She was ready for step two.

Jackson texted his imminent arrival. Jo hurried back to the house and met him in the driveway. She outlined what needed to be done, and he added a couple of useful suggestions. He'd email her the quote as soon as he got back to the office. While in the backyard, she spied an object glinting in the woods. It had not been there when she'd followed the dog previously. Curious, she headed that way, but Flynn hollered for her to join him in the house.

"Landon and I have a question for you. Come upstairs, please."

She followed him and noted he seldom used his cane. Must have his new brace.

Stopping on the landing, he pointed to numerous cans of paint. "Since the painters are coming next week, Landon and I checked the colors for the bedrooms, and we noticed a problem."

"Yeah. They're not all the same color." Landon tapped a can. "Did we make a mistake when we ordered?"

"Nope. The front rooms face south and have large windows. Therefore, the color of the walls will be affected by the amount of light entering. Hence, Morning Sage, a slightly darker shade. As you can tell by the blob on the lid, it's a refined gray with a hint of green. The rooms at the back receive less light, therefore a lighter shade. Misty Sage. The amount of light entering a room must always be considered when choosing wall colors. In my experience, buyers prefer subtle shades that don't dominate a room."

"I told you she'd have a good reason." Flynn set his hands on the toolbelt at his hips. "Besides being a good realtor, she's an interior designer, too."

"The knowledge also comes in handy when staging a home for sale." She seldom bragged, but the way

Flynn boasted about her skills thrilled her no end. In spite of her earlier vow to keep him on a co-worker level, she was amazed at how his compliment and asking her opinion stirred her heart. *Chill, Jo.* Considering her disastrous choice in boyfriends, the last thing she needed was to mess up their friendship.

"By the way, you'll be pleased to note the floral wallpaper is gone."

He remembered her dislike of the blooms. She placed a hand over her heart to settle it's fluttering. "Good riddance. All four bathrooms up here will be painted in pale aqua, which will coordinated with the bedroom colors. For the downstairs bathroom I chose a more vibrant color since it's used by guests. As you might have noticed, the tiles are hand painted Talavera from Mexico—I'm so glad the tenants didn't damage any of them. Lagoon blue walls will emphasize the beautiful artwork."

Landon's phone rang. He retreated to the main bedroom to take the call, and Flynn descended the stairs with Jo.

"Is there a reason you prefer flowers in their natural setting?" He held onto the banister as he negotiated each step.

More memories flooded her mind, but she'd already shared so much with Flynn that she didn't hesitate. "Definitely. The day before our wedding, Phil tried to convince me to elope. Maybe he knew his wife would attend the ceremony. Anyway, he inundated me with bouquets. There must have been a special on Oriental lilies, especially Stargazers. They're pretty—white with intense pink veins down each petal, but I cannot tolerate their scent. I found the smell offensive, cloying, suffocating, and it makes me nauseous. Of course, the bouquets contained other flowers, but that awful odor permeated my apartment, my life, and always reminds me of Phil's duplicity. Ever since then, I rather not have cut flowers in my home. Or depictions of them on the walls."

"I understand." He cleared his throat. "Um, I've deliberately shied away from any reference to our heavy discussion, but I'm curious. How are you dealing with the return of your memories? Your walk with God? Your mother? Especially since she's celebrating a big birthday tomorrow."

At the bottom of the stairs, Jo leaned against the banister and gazed out the large living room windows. "Some memories are still painful, but I wouldn't want to be trapped in the amnesia cave again. I'm relearning how to pray, and I've asked God for forgiveness, but I feel unworthy."

"A common experience for us mortals. But remember, the blood that cleanses our sins has already been shed on the cross. Jesus doesn't have to die repeatedly. But we do need to repent and seek forgiveness. A reminder that we sin and need to work on changing our ways."

"I know, but it's hard to accept God's grace."

"True." He sat on the bottom step. "Excuse me. I've been on my feet too much today. How about Serena. Your mother?"

"I haven't spoken to Serena. Been too busy here. But I'm making progress. Phil emailed me again, but this time I didn't get mad. I suggested we meet. He's in Spokane for a week but can came to Silverdale later." Jo explained her feeble attempts to call Mother. "I'll try to speak to her tomorrow. After the party."

"Good idea. I have a bit of news. Wesley emailed me to say Noah has a new friend at the group home. It's Lewis's stepson who also has Williams syndrome. What do you think of that?"

"Interesting."

"I'll keep in touch with Wesley, but for the sake of Noah and his friend, I won't say anything negative about Lewis." He rubbed his thigh. "I, um, have a confession. After our conversation last Sunday, I realized I've been a hypocrite and that's why Ian hasn't talked to me for four years. I emailed him, acknowledged my behavior, and apologized. When he returns stateside..."

"I hope he contacts you. I'll pray he contacts you."

"Thanks. I'd better get back to work before Landon fires me." Flynn eased up and smiled. "Will you attend our church service this Sunday? No pressure, but I'd like you to."

She nodded. "I have something to check on outside. See you tomorrow." Jo took one step, then turned.

"Hey, I forgot to tell you. Deputy Gordon called a few days ago. The fingerprints on my patio door matched a set from this house. Wade or Rosie."

"I figured one of them was involved. Be careful, please."

"I will." His words added a spring to her steps. She traipsed through the long grass to the wooded area behind the house, keeping the metal object in sight. The closer she drew, the more her stomach muscles clenched. A car. Partially burned. And a hideous odor, like boiled cabbage, only more intense.

Jo peered through the lower branches of a pine tree, shoved them aside, and gasped. A body in the driver's seat. Disfigured, but she could tell it was a woman. Although the clothing was singed, Jo recognized the maroon pantsuit Rosie wore.

Chapter 16

To appease Mother, Jo donned one of the few dresses she possessed. An emerald, green number with a draped neckline and straight skirt. Hair tamed with spray, gold necklace and dangling earrings, tan shoes with three-inch heels. Too bad if she towered over most of the other guests.

Although on their trip to Geena's gym, Jo had refenced the teasing she'd endured during her early schoolyears, she had not shared her negative self-image with Flynn last Sunday. Sure, she'd long ago accepted her height, but she knew she couldn't compare with Serena or Kendall's beauty. She'd been ridiculed in college for trying, and finally gave up. But it still hurt to look in the mirror and not like what she saw. However, after praying for forgiveness, she'd also prayed for acceptance of her body, all five-foot-eleven-inches of it, including her unruly red hair and freckles. She was a child of God, unique in many ways.

Gerry's mouth gaped when she opened her front door, and she beamed. Today, she knew she looked good, and for once, thanked God for her…self.

In a light gray suit and navy tie, sandy hair combed back emphasizing his dark eyes, Gerry would certainly please Mother.

They chatted as he drove to her parents' home, but she couldn't remember much of the conversation. What did that signify about her feelings for Gerry when she was preoccupied with relaying to Flynn details the deputy sheriff shared last night, and her impending talk with Mother?

Guests meandered in the gardens and on the extensive deck. Dad had done a great job of organizing Mother's sixtieth bash. Pink and mauve balloons and streamers decorated arbors and shrubs. Round tables covered in pink cloths dotted the area, and vases of pastel flowers were centered on the head table.

Glass of champagne in hand, Jo introduced Gerry to her folks. Mother, wearing a lilac silk dress, graced him with her charming smile, and even complimented Jo on her appearance. Dad planted a kiss on Jo's forehead then shook Gerry's hand vigorously. "Welcome to our home. We hope you enjoy yourself, and don't let our Jo-Jo take you away too early."

Jo frowned at her father as she pulled Gerry away to meet Kendall and her husband, Ray. This was the first time she'd seen her sister since she regained her memories, and she tried hard not to stare.

After the introductions, Ray said, "Jo, you look stunning."

"I agree. Not only beautiful, but confident and—" Kendy pulled Jo aside and whispered, "Who is this guy? You haven't told me about him. Is he the reason you're glowing?"

She desperately wanted to confide in Kendy, but couldn't. "I'll tell you later, but Gerry's only a friend."

They stepped back to the men and Jo asked, "Where are the kids?"

"Kasi's gone in search of a snack and Blake is…" Kendy scanned the deck, "running around with a bunch of balloons."

"How old are your children?" Gerry slid an arm around Jo's waist.

She tolerated his action but would move as soon as politely possible.

"Kasi's seven and Blake, five. And into every imaginable form of mischief." Ray beamed at his wife. "I don't know how she has the patience to homeschool the tyke."

Mother appeared and asked for Ray's and Kendall's help. They crossed the deck just as Jo spied Flynn and Melanie head straight for her. Again, she made introductions and hid a brief smile as the men eyed each other.

"I've heard so much about you." Melanie squeezed Flynn's arm. The petite brunette looked nothing like her brother.

Jo frowned at her coworker. What had he been saying? To hide her confusion, she said, "Unless he's been bragging about my interior design skills, I wouldn't believe a word he says."

It was Flynn's turn to frown, but Jo ignored him. Instead, she moved away from Gerry's side and pointed to a table behind Flynn. "Excuse us, please. I have important information to give Flynn."

They headed to the empty table and sat. "Deputy Sheriff Gordon called late yestrday and confirmed Rosie was in the car. Of course, the deputy can't provide too many details in the on-going investigation and before autopsy results, but when I pressed, she said the victim had been dead forty-eight hours max."

"So not back when you discovered her blood-soaked scarf?"

"Right. And the car was stolen three days ago. Tire tracks in the mud indicate it was driven into the woods after Thursday's rain. I knew it wasn't there when I followed the little dog last week." Jo gulped and tried to keep her voice even. "The deputy believes Rosie was shot before being burned. Maybe if I'd advertised my presence when I witnessed the argument between Rosie and Wade, she'd still be alive."

Flynn covered her hand with his. "Or they could have attacked you."

"I suppose." She shook her head to ward off the what-ifs and withdrew her hand. "Deputy Gordon added the USB drive I discovered was filled with details of arms sales. I wondered why the tenants had built such a sturdy dock. Now I know. To load or unload their heavy goods and have access to the Hood Canal. Anyway, the flash drive also contained contact information for buyers and listed Boyd Fitzgerald as head of the local unit."

"That's good news. Do the authorities know the whereabouts of this Boyd character?"

"No. Until the investigation is wrapped up, Nelda's property is off-limits again."

"I'll let Landon know. Too bad about Rosie."

Jo leaned back and surveyed the myriad guests. She wondered if she could keep Gerry entertained long enough for the numbers to dwindle to where she'd have a chance to be alone with Mother.

Flynn cleared his throat. "I'm pretty sure I know what's going through your mind. Do you want me with you when you talk to your mother?"

"Thanks, but no. I must do this by myself."

"That means Gerry will have to wait for you. Or I could take you home."

"He's pretty easy going. I'm sure he won't mind."

"How did you meet? You went riding with him, right?"

She frowned and nodded.

Flynn held up his hand. "I'm curious, is all. Not trying to interfere with your life. Just making a comment. But be sure to let me know if he doesn't treat you right."

"Thanks for caring, big brother."

He smirked at her.

Well, if he didn't act like a big brother, she wouldn't have used those word. "I'd better get back to Gerry in case he does take off."

"You look beautiful. He'd be a fool to let you go."

"Now you sound like Mother. You should have seen the gleam in her eye when I introduced him to my folks. I'm sure she heard wedding bells ring and the pitter-patter of little feet."

Flynn scooted back his chair. "Let me know what happens when you talk with her. Wesley's here and I want to speak to him about Lewis. Bye for now." He motioned Melanie to follow him and strode toward a group of people near the head table.

Hmm. He didn't react to Jo's comment about wedding bells. She wasn't sure what she expected. Maybe just a spark of interest. Shrugging, she returned to Gerry.

Dad's voice over the sound system invited guests to be seated, and the festivities began in earnest. His speech touched Jo's heart. He loved Mother, not just evidenced by today's events, but by the way he always treated her with respect, listened to her suggestions about their real estate business. Why hadn't Jo noticed previously? Maybe because of her own negative attitude.

A small orchestra played Mother's favorite classical pieces while waitstaff served the meal. Later, the guests played silly party games. Jo had no idea Mother enjoyed such frivolities. For games like charades and telephone, the guests were divided into groups. The sticky note game required everyone to mingle. Dad placed a note with the name of a celebrity on participants' foreheads. People had to ask fellow guests questions about the person to try to identify the mystery name. Jo never did discover Madame Curie as her celebrity. Musical chairs was the last game, and even the kids abandoned the bouncy house to join in.

Although Gerry rolled his eyes a time or two, he did play along, even for charades which he obviously didn't enjoy. Jo shared the sentiment, but participated because she'd never seen Mother so outgoing and childlike. Considering the joyous atmosphere, there was no way Jo could talk with Mother today.

Their meeting would have to wait even longer. Before Jo left, Dad announced a surprise trip. He and Mother were going on a brief vacation to Victoria, British Columbia.

During the drive home, Gerry reminded Jo of her promise to go out with him next Saturday.

"What are your plans? Riding again, or—"

"Not this time." He turned to her and grinned. "My favorite outdoor activity. Hiking the Wildcat Trailhead. A delicious picnic lunch to follow."

"Sounds wonderful. I haven't tried that trail before, but there are many others around Green Mountain I've ridden."

Gerry had been such a good sport at Mother's party, and Jo did enjoy his company, but he held her hand at times, leaned close to talk to her, especially if Flynn was nearby. She didn't want the relationship to go any further. Saturday's date would be their last.

Sunday dawned overcast and drizzly. Dressed in an ivory silk blouse and cobalt blue slacks with a short-sleeved jacket, Jo drove to the meeting hall and arrived as the worship began. She'd located her Bible and carried it under her arm. This time, Flynn sat at the back and had saved a seat for her.

He smiled as she sat and leaned over to whisper, "I'm pleased you're here. You look radiant."

The compliment caused heat to *radiate* into her cheeks. Throughout the service, she was acutely aware of him beside her. Not only because of his words, but his tenor voice, his bowed head for the prayers, and his nodding or "amens" during the sermon. As the first service she'd been a part of for eight years, she was glad to be sitting with someone who knew of her recent journey back to God, someone from whom she could draw strength.

Sometime in the near future, Jo would tell Mother and Dad she liked their classmate, Pastor Orin Willoughby. He might be short in stature, but his booming voice articulating Biblical truths made him seem ten feet tall.

~

With Nelda's house off-limits, Jo remained in the Silverdale office the next week, concentrating on the closing for the Underwoods' sale, preparing the Adair's house to be advertised to rent, and checking on other rental properties under Tremaine's umbrella. Jackson Reed from the landscape company had emailed a quote which she accepted.

Flynn met with a few clients, but he had his hands full drafting letters to would-be contributors to his motel purchase fund. Jo assisted as time allowed. He wanted the apartments furnished, and she was delighted he asked her to provide her expertise in paint colors, furnishings, and décor.

His self-defense class that week garnered two more students. Jo had already made plans to ride with Vic and Emma through Newberry Hill Heritage Park. Otherwise, she might have attended. Their conversation during the ride had warmed her soul. Vic commented on how relaxed she appeared.

"Either you and Max have set a date, or you dumped him."

"He's out of my life, and so is Serena." Jo explained the reason she transferred to the Silverdale office.

"I'm happy for you." Emma grinned as she added, "Your new boss sounds interesting."

"He is." Jo pedaled ahead of her teammates and was relieved when they reached their vehicles. She didn't want to continue that conversation.

On Wednesday, while busy at her computer, Jo overheard Brian talk with a man in the reception area. The husky-voiced visitor asked to see Flynn. Brian knocked and opened Flynn's door. Curious, Jo scooted her desk chair so she could see the man. Stocky, well-built, disheveled, long gray hair a mess. Flynn left his door ajar, and although Jo continued working, she couldn't help but overhear parts of the conversation.

Cole, a Marine buddy. Down on his luck. Homeless. Nightmares. Flynn explained his plans for the motel and offered Cole a job at Nelda's house. The man accepted the offer. Then he asked after Geena.

Jo's ears perked up, especially when Flynn spoke of her in loving tones.

About that time, Flynn said, "Let's pray together," and closed his door.

The whole incident cemented in Jo's mind that Flynn was a generous, God-fearing man who didn't hide his Christian light under anything.

But why did his words concerning Geena sit so heavy on her heart?

Later that afternoon, Flynn knocked on Jo's office door. "I have an opportunity to meet with a group of potential donors tomorrow. Can you accompany me, please? So far, I've only written letters requesting funds. I'm not sure how to ask people face-to-face."

"Think about the veterans you want to help. Keep their faces in mind and you'll be inspired to ask for millions." Leaning back in her chair, Jo noted Flynn's pleading expression. "I'd be honored to join you."

The meeting resulted in the group agreeing to donate a generous amount. Flynn's buoyant mood lasted the rest of the day.

Saturday rolled around cooler than usual with skies the color of gloom. Gerry decided to go ahead with their plans and Jo agreed. He drove to the Wildcat Trailhead area and parked his pickup in a secluded spot.

Jo peered into the backseat. "I see a backpack. Is our picnic in there?"

"Aha. All a surprise. Let's get going before it rains." He slung the pack onto his shoulder. "I have bottled water if you need a drink before lunch."

About a half mile along the wide track, Gerry took a detour. "There's a beautiful waterfall up ahead. Be careful on the narrow path."

They slogged through the dense undergrowth.

"You call this a path?" She chuckled and stepped over a downed tree trunk, slippery with moss.

"I did say it was narrow. It's been a while since I was here and I'm out of shape. I need a break." He perched on the trunk. "Want a drink?"

"Not yet, thanks." She sat beside him. "Too bad the mountains are shrouded in mist."

After swigging half the water, he smacked his lips. "Yeah, the view from here is incredible." He plucked moss off the tree then turned to her. "Whatever happened to the shoebox you found at that house in my neighborhood?"

During all their time together, he hadn't once asked about Nelda's house. "Why are you interested in a shoebox?"

"Curious if you found anything out of the ordinary

in it."

Strange response. Jo stood and stepped on a rock, losing her balance.

Gerry caught her before she fell down a slope. "Whoa. You okay?"

"Yeah. Thanks. It's drizzling. Should we go back?"

"No. Let's press on to the waterfall." Gerry shoved his bottle back in his pack and returned to the barely discernable path. A few yards ahead, he slipped as he stepped over a clump of wet rocks. He grabbed a jagged branch which slowed his fall, but the broken wood sliced through his wrist. Blood dripped down his arm.

Jo hurried to him. "We must stop the bleeding. Do you have anything in your pack we can use?"

"A light jacket."

She removed the garment and pressed it against the slash. "I'll hold this in place while you get up. Okay?"

But he couldn't stand. His ankle was wedged between two large rocks.

Jo pulled her phone from her pocket. No cell service in the thick forest. "I'll return to the main track and find help. Stay put." She patted his shoulder. "Sorry, wrong thing to say."

"There's a first aid kit in my truck." Hand shaking, he passed her the keys. "I'll keep trying to free my foot."

Holding onto sturdy branches, she made her way back to the track in short order, but found no one to help. She ran to Gerry's truck and hunted for the kit.

Under the seats. In the center console. The glove box. Among a multitude of papers, she located the small, red container. But as she removed it, the registration papers for the vehicle fell out. She picked them up and the name zoomed in and out of focus. Boyd Fitzgerald. Not Gerry Collins. Fitz*gerald*.

Boyd. The leader of the arms smuggling operation.

Blood thudded in her brain as if trying to escape. No wonder he asked about the shoebox. What should she do? He did need medical assistance, but if she returned to him, could she hide the fact she knew his true identity? Call for help? Yes. Sheriff and ambulance. She withdrew her phone again and looked toward the trail.

A man half ran, half hopped down the track. Gerry, uh, Boyd.

She had to leave. Keys? Nowhere to be seen.

Boyd gained on her position, yelling at her. "It's your fault."

Too alarmed to decipher what he meant, she abandoned the vehicle and ran first along the track then into the cleared area and toward the dense woods. She'd make the call when safe.

Boyd started the truck and followed her, the vehicle bouncing over the uneven ground.

She zig-zagged. He kept right behind her, again yelling cuss words mixed with accusations. Time and again she avoided a collision. *Don't look back. Don't look back.* But she couldn't help herself. She turned and tripped. Stumbled and fell. When she righted herself, he rammed into her. Pain shot through her hip, then her shoulder and head when she hit the dirt. She tasted blood mixed with mud.

He reversed and aimed at her again. She attempted to move and couldn't. Weaving in and out of consciousness, she steeled herself against another strike.

Raised voices, then strong arms lifted her. Carried her into the woods.

Silence.

Jo awoke to beeping monitors. Warm, soft bed. And the delicious aroma of coffee. She opened her eyes. Phil, holding a cup of Seattle's Best, sat in a chair beside her bed. She must be dreaming. Blinked. Tried to sit up. The room spun, blood pounded in her head, exacerbating her headache. Rubbing her temple, she focused on Phil. "What are you doing here? Were you following me?"

"Yes. Good thing, too." Phil's raspy voice hadn't changed. "That guy was trying to kill you."

"Oh, yeah. I remember. Where's my phone? I need to make a call." But then the important detail she learned about Gerry slipped from her mind.

"No. You need to rest."

"What's this for?" She pointed to her left arm covered in a sling.

"You had a dislocated shoulder. You have a concussion and severely bruised hip and many scrapes.

The doctor will be in later. She said you were so out of it when she treated you that she didn't review your injuries with you then."

Jo rested against the pillows. Snippets of the past hours faded in and out of her memory. Gerry's injury. His pickup. Arms to the rescue, trip to the ER. Conversations from medical staff. She winched as she remembered the setting of her shoulder. Finally, an elevator ride to this room. "Where am I? I mean, what hospital?"

"St. Michael's, Silverdale. Hope you don't mind, but I called your father. He said he'd notify a man named Flynn. Your phone's on the side table."

Processing the information hurt her brain. Phone. Who was she going to call? Back burner for now. She squinted at Phil and asked, "Why were you at the trail?"

"I need to talk to you. Serena told me about our child."

Eyes wide, Jo glared at Phil and momentarily forgot about her resolve to forgive. What a conniving woman. She opened her mouth to respond, but Mother entered the room.

"Joanna, you and Phil have a *child*?"

Mother's accusatory tone took Jo's breath away.

Chapter 17

Anita and Thomas had entered Jo's room ahead of Flynn. He'd held back so as not to overwhelm the patient and hovered in the hall, waiting to hear Jo's reply. But then he decided she might need a referee, or at least someone in her corner.

He stepped into the crowded room. Anita stood with her hands on her hips. Thomas's gaze flitted from his daughter to the man beside the bed. Jo, face as white as the sheet covering her torso, reached out her free hand to Flynn. He'd noticed the sling, but no cast or visible bandages.

Accepting the invitation, he almost elbowed Anita out of the way and took Jo's hand.

"Mr. McCaul, you don't need to be here."

"Yes, he does, Mother."

"Well." Anita moved a chair to the foot of the bed and sat, face turned away from Jo.

Flynn squeezed Jo's fingers, hoping to encourage her to stick to her goals. He nodded and whispered, "You can do it."

"Serena has caused enough trouble. She lied to you, Phil. Sorry. There is no baby. I had a miscarriage." Jo stared at her mother, probably itching to address the topic Flynn knew ate at her heart.

Anita raised her chin and opened her mouth, but Thomas leaned down and said, "Don't, Anita." He tugged his left earlobe.

The woman blushed and clutched the purse in her lap.

Flynn took control of the situation. "Jo does have more to share, but before she continues, let's hear from Phil regarding Jo's accident." He couldn't believe neither Thomas nor Anita had asked about her injuries. They cared, or they wouldn't be here, and maybe the mention of a child took precedence. Nodding to the hero of the hour, Flynn said, "I believe you brought Jo to the ER?"

The tall, lean man across the room cleared his throat and described how he'd followed Jo, lost sight of her, then saw her again as the guy in the pickup tried to kill her. "I carried her toward the woods, but then the man slowed and stopped. When I checked on him, he appeared to be unconscious, and he'd lost a lot of blood. I disabled his truck, called the sheriff, and brought Jo here. She was my first priority."

"Thank you, Phil." She smiled at him. "I never thought I'd say this, but I'm glad you were here today."

His hand on Anita's shoulder, Thomas echoed the sentiment and added, "So you know who caused the accident, punkin?"

"I do. The date I brought to your party, Mother."

"He seemed like such a nice man. Good looking, polite. Why—?"

"Gerry?" Anger roiled in Flynn's gut.

"I don't wish to discuss him right now." Muscles twitched in Jo's rigid jawline.

Phil walked around the bed and stopped at the door. "Serena lied about so many things. You didn't want to see me, did you?"

Jo shook her head.

"I was hoping to… Never mind. I can see you have other interests." He looked directly at Flynn. "Guess I'll head back to Seattle. Bye, Jo. I wish you all the best."

The man left the room, and Jo blew out a breath.

Flynn studied her. Color had returned to her cheeks, but her lips were drawn in a thin line. A concussion was the least of her problems. The long-overdue talk with Anita loomed, and Flynn was going to make sure it happened today. While he could support her. He squeezed her hand again. Although his leg ached and the sensation of angry ants crawling across his foot and between his toes was about to force him to sit, he refused. He'd stand guard over Jo however long she needed him.

A knock on the door and a petite woman strode into the room. Stern expression on her lined face, hair drawn back in a tight bun. She reminded Flynn of a drill sergeant.

"I'm Doctor D'Spain." Her gruff voice didn't match her size. She eyed the visitors. "The patient needs rest. Don't stay too long." Turning to Jo, she added, "I'm keeping you overnight, maybe longer. You received a nasty concussion, so we'll monitor your symptoms. And I'm concerned about your hip. X-rays showed no fracture, but obviously there's severe bruising. No strenuous physical activity until your regular doctor gives the all-clear. Keep your arm in the sling for at least forty-eight hours. The muscles and soft tissue need time to rest and heal. I've ordered ice packs three times a day. You're very fortunate to have no broken bones. You must be pretty fit." With one last leer at Flynn and Jo's parents, Doctor D'Spain said, "Five more minutes," then she exited the room.

Jo giggled. "I won't argue with her."

Still holding his hand, she gave his fingers a squeeze as if asking him to stay. He opened his mouth to introduce the discussion, but Thomas beat him to it.

"Punkin, we didn't know. Tell us about your miscarriage." He moved to the chair vacated by Phil and sat then kissed Jo on the forehead.

In a detached, cold tone, she described her life after storming out of the church building on her wedding day. When she added she'd suffered from emotional amnesia and only recently unlocked those memoires, Thomas tsked and leaned forward, while Anita appeared unaffected.

Jo hesitated when introducing the topic of the

support group, but then she raised her chin and said, "Robert Latrelle was the counselor."

Anita almost dropped her purse. Thomas whipped his head around to his wife, back to Jo, signifying, in Flynn's estimation, he knew the name.

Pale and lips quivering, Anita narrowed her eyes at her daughter. "Why…why did you mention his name?"

"I think you know. But the big question is, does Kendy?" In obvious distress, Jo swallowed and closed her eyes briefly.

Thomas rose and stood by his wife. "In order for you to make the connection, Robert must have shared too many details about his life. Kendy does not know. I, however, have known all along. Anita told me when I proposed."

Squirming against the pillows as if uncomfortable, Jo released Flynn's hand and pushed the button to raise the head of her bed. "Are you ever going to tell her?"

Anita glanced up at Thomas. He shook his head. "We were not." He tugged his earlobe again. "And you don't have to."

Jo pawed at her sheet. "I…I won't, but I think you're being unfair to her."

"Your mother and I will determine whether or not we discuss the issue with Kendall."

A nurse bustled in with pain meds and an icepack which he placed on Jo's shoulder. While administering the meds to the patient, he said, "I'll be back for the icepack in fifteen minutes. A reminder from Doctor

D'Spain. One visitor can stay as long as Jo gets some rest." On his way out, he closed the door.

"I have one more topic to address, then, Mother and Dad, you can leave. I'd like Flynn to stay."

Jo's words did a number on his heart and his pulse raced. Certain she was safe now, Flynn drew a chair close and sat. He rubbed his thigh then his shin, but the massage did little to chase away the ants.

"I agree it's not my place to tell Kendall, but I have to know, Mother, why have you always treated me like I'm the…the…child with a different father? That I'm the result of your, um, indiscretion?"

Anita blushed. She looked at Jo and shook her head. "That's just not true."

This time, Jo made a fist and pounded the bed. "Let me remind you. You criticize me at every turn. My preference in clothing, my unruly hair. Even the color, as if I chose it. Wait, wait." She held up her hand when Anita opened her mouth. "Why didn't I get a degree in business, like Kendy? When am I getting married? Why won't I give up my cycling to appease a suitor? Why…?" Voice breaking, Jo shrank among the pillows, moisture pooling in her eyes.

If only Flynn could take her in his arms. Instead, he handed her a tissue then brushed her curls, her vibrant red curls, off her forehead. He was about to suggest Thomas and Anita leave, when the woman stood and fiddled with her purse strap. "I'm sorry my actions and words have hurt you, Joanna dear. But you see, I never loved Robert, and whenever I see Kendy's resemblance to him, I guess I overcompensate and shower her with compliments."

Jo grabbed Flynn's hand and squeezed so hard he thought she'd cut off the circulation to his fingers. Anita's explanation didn't seem to assuage her deep hurt. He couldn't blame her.

No one spoke, not even Thomas. He didn't go to Anita's defense. In fact, he seemed detached, aloof, as if the rift between his wife and daughter was none of his business. Feeling a bit awkward witnessing the drama, Flynn looked toward the door. "Maybe you both should leave now."

Jo's complexion took on a grayish hue and she appeared as unyielding as a statue.

At the door, Anita turned. "Joanna, can you forgive me?"

"Your explanation sounds plausible, but it doesn't address why you treated me like the ugly stepdaughter. I'll think about forgiveness, but please go now. I have a headache."

Thomas kissed his daughter again, placed his arm around Anita's shoulders, and they left the room.

As the only person who seemed concerned about Jo's physical condition, Flynn stroked her hand, hoping she'd release the vise grip. She did, and he asked, "Are the pain meds kicking in?" He couldn't protect her from Gerry, but he could take care of her needs.

She nodded. "I'm thirsty. For hot coffee because

I'm cold. Not just on the outside, but in my soul. As if I spent a decade in the Arctic."

Flynn pulled up the blanket and draped it over her. "I'll check with the nurse to make sure you have no dietary restrictions, then I'll see what the cafeteria offers. How about food?"

"Yeah. I missed lunch. A sandwich or fruit." She giggled again, but the sound soon turned into a wail of anguish.

Flynn stood and took her in his arms as much as her injured shoulder allowed. She didn't weep, but her body shuddered and eventually, she exhaled a woeful sigh. He held her a minute longer, then withdrew his arms. "I'll be back soon. Then you need to sleep. I'll stay with you a while."

She didn't respond, but her smile warmed his heart. With the nurse's approval, he hurried to the cafeteria, purchased two cups of hot chocolate, a container of fresh fruit chunks, and two club sandwiches.

Prepared to tease her about no caffeine allowed, he elbowed open the door, but Jo was asleep. He set the items on the tray table and settled in the recliner in the corner. When he'd received the call from Thomas, he'd been in the middle of a workout and hadn't had lunch, either. The hot chocolate and sandwich barely touched sides. He was about to raise the leg rest when Jo's phone chirped. He retrieved it and stepped into the hall. Caller ID named Sheriff Gordon.

"Hello. I'm Flynn McCaul, Jo's a colleague."

"I know who you are, Mr. McCaul. How's Jo? Are you with her?"

"Yes. She's asleep." He described her injuries. "Doc wants to keep her in at least until Monday. She knows who ran her down. Is the man in custody?"

"Yes. Boyd Fitzgerald is the—"

"She said it was Gerry. I don't remember his last name."

"No, our identification is correct. He has a long criminal record, and we're sure he's the leader of the gun smuggling operation. We were able to lift Wade's fingerprints from the car where Rosie died." The woman paused, then added, "Please give Jo my best and tell her we'll get her statement later."

Flynn slipped Jo's phone into his shirt pocket and entered the room then halted. *Boyd Fitzgerald, not Gerry?* Brain cells ticked over. Then he made the connection. Gerry. Fitzgerald. Poor Jo. Another loser boyfriend. He'd have to find out how they met.

Before returning to his seat, he watched her sleep. Her face was relaxed, and no one observing her would imagine the emotional and physical turmoil she'd endured. He gently tucked the blanket up to her neck and whispered, "Jo, you are not the ugly stepsister. In my eyes, you're beautiful."

She stirred and he backed up. Had she heard him?

"Hey, Errol Flynn, thanks for staying. I...I..." She drifted back to sleep.

What was she about to say? Flynn kissed her on the

cheek. As he settled in the recliner, he whispered, "Why did you call me Errol Flynn?"

Chapter 18

At four in the morning, Flynn returned home. Jo had slept most of the night, and with Boyd in custody, she was safe. The recliner had offered minimal comfort, but Flynn's leg ached, and he needed to take his meds before the pain reached unbearable levels. He slept a few hours in his comfortable bed, showered, ate a decent breakfast, then headed downtown to purchase a gift for Jo. No flowers or fruit basket. Leave those for other visitors who might not know about her aversion to cut flowers. He wanted a gift that was personal without being *too* personal.

He scoured the shelves in the bookstore until he found the perfect item. Seated in his pickup, he placed the book beside the slab of dark chocolate in the small gift bag he'd brought and covered it with tissue paper. At the hospital, he purchased a large cup of her favorite coffee and headed to her room.

In the hallway leading to her door, he met Kendall and Ray.

Ray shook Flynn's hand and said, "Good to see you

again. Jo told us how you helped her yesterday."

"She appreciated your support in keeping her grounded while she told Mom and Dad about her miscarriage." Kendall slipped her arm through Ray's. "And later, the hot chocolate and sandwich."

Good. So, Jo had shared part of her conversation.

Kendall noted Flynn's gift bag. "Hmm. No flowers. You must know my sister well. We gave her a neck massager."

Not sure how to respond, Flynn pointed toward Jo's room. "I'm curious to see if she likes my alternate choices."

"Thanks again. We're off to church. Good luck convincing Jo to stay another day. She's ready to go home." Kendall tugged at her husband's arm, and they proceeded down the hall.

Flynn knocked on Jo's door and poked his head around.

Smiling, she beckoned him in.

He set the bag on the side table along with the coffee and his Bible and cradled her extended hand. A purple bruise on her left temple renewed his anger toward Gerry. Boyd. "You're looking better this morning. How's the shoulder and hip?"

"Wish I could say all's well, but I ache all over. My brain feels as if it's going to burst out of my skull and run for the hills."

"Yeah. I can empathize. I've had a concussion and it takes a while for the swelling to go down."

"I see you brought me coffee. Thank you. Please pass me the cup. It hurts to move."

He made sure she had a good grip on the cup before he removed his fingers. Leaning back in the chair, he kept his eyes on her. Bruised, in pain, no makeup, hair a mess, hospital gown askew around her neck. She'd never looked more beautiful. He cleared his throat and picked up the gift bag.

"Mmm. Delicious." Jo closed her eyes and took another swallow of coffee.

"I'm glad you're enjoying the drink, but I have something else for you." He was anxious to see her reaction to the book.

She handed him the cup and took the bag, tossing aside the tissue paper. "Yum. My favorite chocolate, and a book. *Dogs are Hilarious.* This looks like fun." She tried to hold it and flip pages, but gave up. "You read it to me."

Flynn scooted his chair so he could hold the book in front of her and read the captions. "These are photos of rescue dogs caught in unusual or weird poses." He showed her each page and read the words. Before he was halfway through, she asked him to stop. Laughing hurt too much. He moved the tray table closer to her and set the book and coffee cup within her reach, beside the opened massager box. The item occupied a chair while charging.

"Kendall says you're itching to go home."

"I am. She knows me well and brought a change of

clothes and my phone charger. But I will be a good little patient and listen to my doctor. The nurse did get me up earlier and I walked up and down the hall." Jo sipped more coffee.

Eager to ask about Boyd, but hesitant to alter the companionship developing between them, he examined the massager's instruction booklet. "Have you used one of these before?

She shook her head. "Not one this fancy. Ray said after his left rotor cuff surgery last year, his neck and right shoulder muscles became so tight because they compensated for his injury. By the way, Doctor D'Spain visited earlier and agreed I could use the massager sparingly for now."

He could delay no longer. "While you slept yesterday, I took a call from the sheriff. She said Boyd was in custody and she confirmed he's the head of the arms smuggling group."

Jo sighed. "Yeah, that's why he tried to kill me. I discovered Gerry was an alias for Boyd Fitzgerald. I feel like a fool. He certainly hoodwinked me." She frowned and then her eyes bugged. "I just remembered what he shouted at me as he tried to run me over. I was to blame for Rosie's death. Wade killed her because she didn't support him. My fault because I found the ammo and thumb drive." Slumping against the pillows, she grimaced as the movement probably aggravated her shoulder.

"Jo, it's not your fault. You have nothing to feel

guilty about. It might be trite to say, but bad people do bad things." Flynn removed her coffee cup from her grasp and set it on the tray. "How…how did you meet Boyd?"

"At Nelda's house the first time I visited. In the driveway. He pretended to be a concerned resident in the neighborhood. I gave him a business card in case he heard of anyone interested in purchasing the property. Another one bites the dust." She turned her head and faced the window.

"He certainly was charming when we met at your mother's party. I can—"

"Don't give me any sympathy. It's time I accepted the fact I have no sense when it comes to choosing men to date. I'm going to be a spinster aunt all my life."

Flynn couldn't tell if she was joking or serious. Maybe the pain meds were kicking in. She closed her eyes, and all he could think to say was, "Would you like me to leave?"

"No, please don't go. You might not be a professional counselor, but I need counseling."

"I'll stay as long as you need me. I can offer advice, pray with you. And I brought my Bible."

"Good. Please pray that I can forgive Mother because after her reaction yesterday, I'm not sure I'm a strong enough person. Her reasons for treating me differently didn't make sense yesterday, and upon reflection today, I feel the same way. Especially after seeing Kendall. I love and admire her, and maybe she's just a nicer, more likeable person than I am."

"Whoa, Miss Tremaine." He gestured a timeout. "I'll admit you and your sister have very different personalities, as do Ian and I, me. Whatever. Don't take that as a negative. Kendall may not have been teased about her height or red hair, but you are a strong woman, in part because of what you endured. You are you, and you must not try to change your personality to suit other people, to meet their expectations. Wouldn't the world be a boring place if we were all the same?"

Finally, she faced him again and smiled. Then giggled. "That's funny. Lots of little Flynns running around. Tall redheads cycling the globe. I'd have saved myself a heap of trouble if I only had you to…" Her smile slipped from her lips and her cheeks reddened.

He pretended not to understand the direction her thoughts were taking and changed the subject. "Last night, you awoke at some point and called me Errol Flynn. I'd like to know why?"

"I did?" She rubbed her temple. "You're making my brain hurt by expecting me to remember what I said while under the influence of a controlled substance."

"No, no, young lady, you can't blame the meds. The name slipped off your tongue too easily, as if you'd used it many times. I won't leave this room until you tell me." He crossed his arms and leaned back.

"Okay, I won't sugarcoat my reason. Dad has hired many former Marines and not all were successful. Seriously, one guy didn't know how to turn on a computer. Also, keep in mind, I'd just returned from a fabulous vacation, but Serena had purloined a lucrative sale, and mother was on my case because I'd rejected Max and my hair was a disaster and my clothes a disappointment. When dad informed me about another Marine, Flynn McCaul the tech genius who was going to transform our programs, I might have mentally coined the phrase 'Errol Flynn to the rescue'." She squinted at him. "I might have thought about you that way until I attended your presentation."

He nodded, scratched his chin, keeping her waiting a few more seconds. "So, actually a compliment?"

"Yes." She tossed the massager instruction booklet at him. "I can see you're trying hard not to laugh. And here I thought I'd offended you."

"It'll take a lot more than a nickname to hurt my feelings. But, hey, we're getting off track." He took her hand. "I'd like to pray."

"Okay."

"Father, God, help us to live as recipients of Your abundant grace and forgive us when we doubt Your acceptance of Your repentant children. Give Jo strength to forgive her mother and understanding in how to forge closer bonds with her. Thank You that Phil was on hand to assist Jo, and we're also thankful she was not seriously injured. Please help her to realize her uniqueness. In Jesus' name. Amen."

Reluctant to release her hand, Flynn kept his head bowed until she pulled away.

"Thanks. Your words of advice sound a lot like counseling to me. I appreciate your wisdom."

"I haven't said anything that's not addressed in the Bible." Although her comments sat well with him, he didn't respond, but picked up his copy from the table. "There are so many Scriptures I could read to encourage you, but I want to focus an old favorite—Psalm 23."

"I had to memorize it one time in Sunday School, and I can still recite it."

"Good. I chose this passage because weeks ago you referred to yourself as a lost sheep, and I asked if you were ready to return to the Shepherd. David, the Psalmist, uses word pictures to describe how our heavenly Shepherd takes care of us. We can rely on Him—"

A knock on the door and an aide arrived with Jo's lunch tray.

"That time already. I'd better go. We can continue the study another time." Flynn lifted the cloche over the plate and sniffed the savory aroma of Salisbury steak and gravy.

"Why don't you visit the cafeteria and bring your lunch up here?" Jo adjusted her sling.

"Good idea." He stepped toward the door, but Thomas entered, carrying a large bouquet of pink and lilac flowers, and a large, silver Get Well balloon covered in pink hearts.

"Hi, punkin. Flynn." He walked around the bed and

kissed Jo on the forehead. "How are you today?" Turning, he set the vase on the wide windowsill then sat on the edge of the bed.

"My mind isn't as foggy, but every muscle hurts. Thanks for the flowers."

"Mother chose them."

Flynn figured as much. Colors Anita favored.

"Where's she?"

"In the car. She, um, wasn't sure if you were ready to see her."

Jo looked at Flynn, eyes wide.

"Maybe when Jo is in a less vulnerable place, physical and emotionally, she'd be ready."

Jo nodded, as if to tell him he'd given Thomas the correct response.

"I'm glad you came, Dad."

He patted her knee. "I knew Mother seemed to favor Kendall and of course I was aware of her criticism of you. I should have stepped in, but you always gave the impression you handled the digs by not altering your behavior. I'm sorry I was mistaken. You've been hurt and I can't erase that experience, but I hope I made up for it by how I treated you, punkin." He tugged on his ear lobe.

Jo swiped at a tear trickling down her cheek. "Oh, Dad. Yes, you've always been my hero, and I remember many times when you took my side in disagreements." She reached across and took his hand. "I love you, Dad."

"And I love you, sweet child."

Flynn swallowed, hard. He was heartened by witnessing the moment and almost added his own sentiment, but held back. Not the right time or place.

Turning to Flynn, Thomas said, "I want to chat with Jo alone. Would you mind? Thank you for your support of her."

Although Flynn wanted to stay, he'd been there over two hours and had enjoyed every minute. He closed his Bible and stood. "I'll be back tomorrow." With the desire to protect her long-term in his heart, he stopped at the door and added, "I still think you should take my self-defense classes."

Instead of dismissing his suggestion, she waved, a smile on her beautiful lips.

Chapter 19

Another hallway walk, more ice packs on her shoulder, vitals checked a dozen times, it seemed, and a visit from Emma and Vic filled the remainder of Jo's day. She went to sleep with words from Flynn's conversation and Dad's reassurances on her heart.

Doctor D'Spain stopped by mid-morning the next day and left Jo with the good news she would be discharged after lunch. Although her shoulder pain had eased, she needed help dressing. Later, she sat in the recliner, and while waiting for her discharge paperwork, flipped through TV channels. One news item caught her attention. A major arms smuggling ring had been busted and the major participants arrested. *Boyd and Wade. Were there any others?*

Jo leaned back and closed her eyes. The end of one nightmare. No more break-ins or collisions with pickup trucks. "Thank You Father for keeping me safe." She paused. "Help me deal with, communicate with my mother in a rational way. Amen." Although not in the same category as a bad dream, talking with Mother might be harder than running away from Boyd.

Her phone rang indicating Flynn as the caller, elevating her mood. "Office of injured co-workers. How may I direct your call?"

He bellowed. "You must be feeling better."

"I am. Going home soon."

"Great. More good news. The sheriff called and Nelda's house has been released."

"I figured as much." Jo provided details from the TV report she'd watched. Flynn didn't say anything right away, so she asked, "Are you Okay?"

"Yeah. Just contemplating life choices and how they affect us."

"Rosie's been on my mind. And her daughter, Molly."

"I'll add the child to my prayer list." He cleared his throat. "Do you need a ride home? I have meetings with clients all day, but I can reschedule."

"Thanks, but no. Kendy's coming."

"Take care. Call if you need anything and don't come back to work too soon. I'm on good terms with the boss and can convince him to fire you."

Jo's turn to laugh. "Ooooh. Shuddering in my boots, um, sneakers. Thanks for yesterday. Bye." She ended the call before the pent-up emotion distorted her voice. Flynn's counsel had gone a long way to soothe her resentment toward her mother, but she needed time to heal physical and emotionally.

Discharge instructions in hand, lunch tray

abandoned, Jo waited for her sister, pacing the room or glancing out the window. She took the opportunity to call Yards Galore, the landscape company, to let them know they could begin work on Nelda's property.

Twenty minutes later, Kendy and her two children entered. "Sorry we're late. There was a wreck close to the Narrows Bridge."

"I'm glad you brought the kids." Jo held out her good arm for hugs from Kasi and Blake.

Kasi pointed to the sling. "Does it hurt?"

"Just a little. Here, can you carry this little bag for me?"

The child took Flynn's bag and smiled at her brother.

"What can I take?" he asked.

Jo untied the balloon from the bouquet and handed it to Blake. "Hold tight. Okay?"

He grinned and headed to the door.

Kendy carried the vase and the massager, and, having dismissed the use of a wheelchair, Jo held on to the hospital-issued plastic bag containing her stained clothes as she walked to the car.

The balloon almost caused a riot in the backseat while Kendy drove to Jo's apartment. As soon as she opened her front door, the kids ran to the toy chest she kept for them in the living room. She took the gift bag down the hall and sank onto her bed. The exertion and anticipation of being home tired her out. "Thanks for the ride, sis."

"No problem. I promised the kids a visit to the Naval Under Sea Museum in Keyport. Since it's only a few miles away, today seemed like a great opportunity for a fieldtrip." She rearranged a few blooms in the vase. "I know how you feel about fresh flowers. What should I do with them?"

"Put the vase on the kitchen counter, please. I…I'm trying to be more tolerant of Mother's actions. According to Dad, she chose the bouquet. After all, isn't that what you do for someone in the hospital? However, she stayed in the car yesterday when he visited."

Kendy delivered the flowers, then joined Jo on the bed. "I've never understood why she's always treated you differently. I'm glad you were brave enough to confront her. How did she react to your miscarriage?"

Words revealing Mother's indiscretion clogged in Jo's throat. She swallowed, coughed to catapult them away. The revelation wasn't hers to share. Exchanging her frown for a smile, Jo selected her words with care. "You can imagine Mother was incredulous. She said little to me because Dad told her to hush. But, by the outraged expression on her face, you'd think no one ever got pregnant before marriage, and that it was my fault the baby didn't survive." Determined not to allow the resentment to fester, Jo skipped over much of the conversation between her and her folks. "I'm sure we will revisit the topic again."

Kendy stood. "I need to leave to give us a couple of

hours in the museum." She noticed the gift bag on the side table. "So, what did Flynn give you?"

"Chocolate and a cute book." Jo withdrew the book and handed it to her sister.

She flipped through the pages and then bopped Jo on the head. "He knows you well. And you have a nice, rosy blush mixing with your freckles and the bruise on your temple." She placed the book on the bed. "Anything I should know about?"

Jo took Kendy by the arm and escorted her from the room. "I like him, but he's my boss and—"

"Really? Some boss to spend the night in the recliner and then to withstand Mother's forceful personality for you."

No response at the ready, Jo pointed to the front door "Thanks again for coming. Now, take your children to the museum."

Once Jo had her apartment to herself again, she heated a mug of water and added a spearmint teabag. Not her favorite drink, but the doctor told her to limit her caffeine while still dealing with headaches and dizziness. Resting on the sofa, she reviewed Kendy's comments about Flynn. Yes, he had shown her great care and consideration, but he might have done the same for Ethan or Brian.

Jo was anxious to get back to work on Nelda's property, at least to supervise the landscapers as Flynn and Landon had the repairs well in hand. *I hope they don't complete the project before I can return.* The bruises on her hip were a psychedelic mix of colors and tender to the touch, and her shoulder ached. The massager did help ease the tightness in her neck, and her lacerations were healing. But her heart hurt. Boyd's dating her only to get the thumb drive back combined with the emotional trauma Mother sent her way, slashed at the very core of her inner being.

Swallowing the last of her tea, Jo stood, chin up, hand on her hip. She would not allow any negativity to get the best of her. Finally, Serena had no hold over her, Mother and Dad knew the truth and she knew the truth about Mother and Robert. Property sales were generating a good income to pay off her debt. She felt more at ease receiving genuine praise from a man, namely Flynn, and she was slowly rediscovering her relationship with God. Jo rinsed the mug and set it in the dishwasher. Flynn. Yeah, she liked working with him. In fact, she liked him. Period.

The next morning before Jo had even taken a shower, her doorbell rang. She almost choked on a mouthful of decaf coffee when she checked the peephole. Mother. She'd never been to Jo's apartment before.

One quick scan of the living room. Presentable. Jo opened the door, and Mother entered, eyeing the compact room. Jo had kept some of her furniture and décor from her former life and was sure Mother wouldn't find anything to criticize.

"How are you feeling, Joanna?" Mother sat on the

edge of the sofa, smoothing her cream-colored skirt over her knees.

"Better, thank you. A good night's rest helped. Would you like a cup of coffee?"

"No. I just had breakfast."

They'd seldom had a tête-à-tête, and Jo almost giggled at the awkwardness between them. Since mother had initiated the meeting, Jo waited for her to continue.

"Um, I'll get straight to the point. I've come to apologize again."

Seated in the armchair, Jo glanced at her immaculately dressed mother. Did she have more to say? Apparently not. Ready to spar, Jo took in a breath instead. "Thank you." She didn't want to accuse her mother of lying, but the reason she'd given in the hospital for treating her and Kendy differently didn't address the topic completely.

"Is that all you have to say?"

Biting her bottom lip, Jo took a moment to reply. "I accepted your apology. What more do you want?"

"Well, um, why don't you consider changing your outlook on life? For instance, I've always thought you don't make the most of your assets. You seldom dress in feminine attire."

"I would look ridiculous in flouncy, floral dresses."

"No, not that. Let me introduce you to my fashion consultant. There's more to looking feminine that fancy dresses."

This time Jo giggled. So that's why Mother always looked perfectly turned out. "I don't think so."

Anita crossed her ankles and tilted her head. "Moving on."

Aware her rejection of her mother's offer perturbed her, Jo also tilted her head, ready for the next onslaught.

"You're too assertive. Most men don't admire that quality in a wife. And, unless you find a husband in your bike club, I suggest you quit. You're too involved and—"

Jo had heard enough. She stood, and fist clenched, paced to the door and back, giving her time to marshal her thoughts and not spew out the anger boiling in her heart. "You say you showered praise on Kendall because of her parentage, but you've never had a kind word for me. From elementary school onward, I don't recall one time you congratulated me for winning a race. Or said you were proud of me for good grades." Jo sat in the other armchair as far away from Mother as possible. "I can't help how I look. I'm not Kendall, I'm not a sweet, pliable woman. And I'm not the boy you so wanted."

"That was uncalled for."

"Tough. It's the truth. Long ago, I overheard you say as much to Dad."

Anita shifted in the chair as if ready to get up.

"I have more to say. This is my life, and if I attract a man, it will be because of who I am and how I dress and what I do, and not to please you and give you more grandchildren."

"You haven't exactly been successful in that endeavor. Phil, Max, this Gerry person. Those are the boyfriends I know about. And don't forget your business partner."

Wow, Mom. You know how to twist the knife. "I admit I've made poor choices, but I've learned a lot from my mistakes." *And still learning.*

"I sure hope so. Why haven't you taken advantage of the men I've introduced to you?" Anita shook her head. "I just want you to be happy and to fulfill your role as a woman."

Energy spent, Jo rolled her eyes. She could argue with her mother's words, but chose to ignore the statement. "I think you should leave, Mother. We may never see eye to eye on anything, and I don't want your advice on how to live my life."

"I was only trying to help." Anita stood, and clutching her leather purse, stepped toward the door. "This is why you believe I treat Kendall differently. She accepts my advice and values my opinion, and I enjoy her company. We never argue and I don't have any reason to criticize her."

"That might be the most truthful thing you've said this morning. Kendy epitomizes femininity. She's petite, beautiful, successful. And she has children. She's the perfect daughter." Jo opened the door. "I love my sister and I wouldn't want her to change one iota, but I can never be her."

Mother stepped out then turned. "I do love you."

Leaning against the closed door, Jo whispered, "Then why have you never shown it?"

~

Headache and dizziness gone, sling discarded, Jo ventured out the next afternoon and called Brian to get Flynn's address. She wanted to discuss Mother's visit away from the office and drove to his condo after giving the sheriff her statement concerning Boyd's assault on her.

Flynn opened the door dressed in shorts and a tank top and barefoot. "Oops. I thought you were delivering my supper. I'll run and put on a shirt."

When he returned, Jo said, "I couldn't help but notice your scars. From the explosion?"

"Yeah." He buttoned the shirt. "Sorry you had to see them."

"But I bared my scarred soul to you. It's only fair. Sort of."

"I suppose. Have a seat. Can I get you a soda or something?" Flynn settled in his recliner.

"No thanks. I won't stay long. Mother visited yesterday, ostensibly to apologize again, but proceeded to tell me how I should change my life." Jo added details from the conversation. "She even threw failed relationships at me. As if I needed reminders."

"How did her visit make you feel?"

"Angry, hurt, but she doesn't understand that no matter how much I change, I can't be a replica of

Kendall." Rubbing her sore shoulder, she added, "Actually, I feel good today. I voiced my opinion and although she may still try to interfere, I'm not going to let her affect my life. She's my mother and I will respect her, but my choices are between me and God." Jo nodded once. Enough said.

"I'm proud of you for keeping your cool in spite of the negativity." He shifted his right leg over his left as if trying to hide the shriveled calf.

Jo pointed at his legs. "I just got through telling Mother to accept me as I am. Your past injuries are part of who you are, Errol Flynn. Don't be ashamed of them."

He blew out a breath. "Not ashamed. Embarrassed, more like it. But I agree." He moved his right leg and spread out his arms. "This is me. Take it or leave it."

Extending one arm, Jo added, "Same here."

They grinned at each other, and a companionable silence filled the room.

With no makeup on, she figured her blush helped conceal her bruised temple. Flynn had shown so much compassion toward her, and if she wasn't mistaken, maybe even a hint of a romantic interest. Her pulse rate increased. She'd found a man she could trust, someone whose company she enjoyed way more than she cared to admit. At least not until she was sure he reciprocated the feelings.

Although Jo had shared details of Mother's visit, she still had one issue to address. "Sorry to take up more of your time, but I want your opinion on my conversation with Mother. Was I too harsh? I have forgiven her, but I don't feel all warm and gooey inside and I don't want to spend hours with her."

"I'm going to add to what we discussed in the restaurant a while back. These statements are about forgiveness in general, not specific to you and Anita. Forgiving a person includes the idea you wish them no harm, you won't hold their acts or words against them. It does not mean you have to seek their company, become best buds, or surrender yourself to their ideas." He leaned forward, elbows on knees. "Maybe for the first time, you told your mother how you really felt and stood up for yourself. From now on, she might respect you more."

"Really?"

"You might not see the results right away. After all, she's had years of practice, but give her time."

The doorbell rang. Flynn rose and limped to the door and received a delivery of savory-smelling items. Jo's mouth watered as she'd had little to eat all day.

"Thanks." He closed the door and carried the bag to the kitchen. "Would you like to stay for the best Thai food I've found in Silverdale? There's plenty as I always order enough for a second meal."

"Yes, thank you."

Flynn set out the containers on his small dining table, and included plates, and glasses of water. They ate and chatted, Mother's visit forgotten for the moment.

"I've had a couple more emails from Wesley. He's doing well, and his wife's condition seems to have stabilized."

"That's great news. I should have communicated with him. What about Noah?"

"He's coping with the new situation and often talks about Lewis, but doesn't mention his stepson much. I find that interesting."

"Since I can't participate in the bike club's ride this weekend, I might visit Wesley and Iris in Tacoma. I can stop by Kendy's home, too." Jo sipped her Tom Yum soup and eyed Flynn through her lashes. "Would you like to join me?"

"Yes."

No hesitation. A good sign.

"We've almost completed the work on Nelda's property so I should be free."

"Which reminds me, I need to stop by to check on the landscaping."

"Yeah. They worked all day yesterday. The gardens are looking good."

Jo helped Flynn clear away the containers, plates, and glasses. "Thanks again for being my sounding board since you won't let me call you my counselor." She picked up her purse. "And for the meal. I need to go home and take pain meds."

"Before you go, I want to show you my progress in the motel purchase." He led the way to his office, taking big strides in spite of his limp. "By the way, one of the guys I served with visited the office last week. Cody Cole. I should have introduced him, but I didn't think he wanted to be seen in that state. I gave him a job at Nelda's place. Cole's had it pretty rough and I want him to be the first vet I help." Flynn sorted through papers on the desk. "Ah, here's my letterhead stationary. I'll send personal letters to all individuals or organizations who've donated funds."

She set her purse on the chair and took the paper. "This looks great. I'll help any way I can. How far along is the campaign?"

"I've secured almost two-thirds of the money needed." Flynn set his hands on his hips, grinning like a proud papa.

The office window faced the front of the condo and Jo noticed a Kitsap County Sheriff's department car pull up to the curb. "Wonder who's in trouble?"

Flynn stepped to the window and shrugged. Then the doorbell rang, and a knock sounded. Jo arrived at the door first, but waited for Flynn to open it.

Two deputies she didn't recognize stood outside, grim expressions on their faces. So, the visit was not Boyd related.

"Flynn McCaul, I'm Deputy Unger and this is my partner Deputy Lennox. May we come in?" the burly male asked.

Stepping aside, Flynn said, "Of course. What's wrong?"

Unger fingered the handcuffs on his duty belt. "I need you to come with us to the station."

"What?" He glared at the officers, then at Jo. "Why?"

"For questioning in relation to the murder of Geena Pierce."

Face pale, Flynn staggered backward until he hit the back of the recliner. "I don't understand."

The female deputy grasped Flynn's arm.

"Wait, please." Jo almost laid a hand on Deputy Lennox but held back when the officer glared at her. "Can't you see his injuries? He needs his leg brace and special shoes and cane."

Flynn raised his eyebrows briefly at her as if to say *thanks.*

"Where are these items?" Unger stepped toward the hall.

"In my bedroom. First door on the left. And my cane is in the office."

"Okay. I'll go with you."

The officer followed Flynn down the hall. He limped more than usual, and Jo wondered if stress made his leg hurt or if he exaggerated the hitch in his gait for the officers' benefit.

Jo acted as nonchalantly as she knew how and studied the photos on the mantel. The good-looking man in uniform must be Ian.

Now wearing jeans and his shoes, and gripping his cane, Flynn entered the living room. "I'm saddened by the news of Geena's death, but I haven't seen her in four years. Why do you need to question me?"

"If you don't come voluntarily, we will arrest you." Lennox waved a piece of paper under Flynn's nose. "By the way, we have a warrant to search your condo. Let's go." She jutted her head toward Jo. "That includes you, ma'am."

"I'm Jo Tremaine. But I need to get my purse from the office."

"Fine. I'll come with you." She glared at her partner and followed Jo.

Minutes later, purse in hand, Jo stood on the sidewalk biting her lip.

Positioned in the back seat, Flynn gave her a brief smile.

After the sheriff's vehicle exited the complex, Jo reached into her purse for her keys and found Flynn's phone. Why did he slip it in there when he collected his cane?

Chapter 20

The only time Flynn came close to seeing the inside of a cell occurred during his second year of service in the US Marines. And, so far, he'd only been hauled away in a squad car, and now sat in an interview room, waiting on his lawyer. He prayed he wouldn't call a cell home today, either. Deputy Lennox had confiscated Flynn's cane as if he might use it as a weapon. He stretched his legs under the metal table and looked at the glass panel in the door every time someone walked past. Thomas admitted he was shocked by Flynn's phone call, but promised to contact a lawyer right away.

Although his palms began to sweat and a wave of heat trickled through his body, Flynn closed his eyes, determined not to give in to the panic. He recalled Jo's face, the curve of her lips. His breathing slowed as the door opened.

Detective Elliot, who had talked with Flynn earlier, entered the room and sat at the table. "Your lawyer's on her way. Do you need anything?" He patted his combed-over hair which didn't do much to hide his baldness.

"Only answers to my questions. When did Geena die? Where was she found? Why do you think I'm responsible?"

"I didn't say you were responsible." The man leaned back and balanced the rickety chair on two legs.

A person his size ought to be more careful. Any minute, Flynn could see the chair buckle under his weight. He shook off the distraction. "Why am I here, then?"

Elliot righted the chair and set his elbows on the table. "All in good time."

A knock on the door.

"Your lawyer, I presume." Elliot let in a statuesque blonde woman, probably in her late fifties, indicating she might have lots of experience.

"I need time with my client." She handed him a business card.

"Ten minutes, Miss Miller." The detective left the room.

"Gail Miller, Flynn. So, tell me why you're here?" She sat beside him.

"I'm not sure. Yes, Geena Pierce and I were engaged, but I haven't seen her in years. And I certainly didn't kill her. They haven't told me anything about her murder. Do you have details?"

"A few. She was found in the woods near your condo, apparently holding your dog tags."

"No. Not possible. My tags are in a trunk in my living room with all my other military gear. I use it as a coffee table. Do you know when the murder occurred?"

"They haven't shared that detail with me. But when the detective returns, only answer questions I deem appropriate. Ready?"

"I suppose. Thanks for coming at such short notice."

"The Tremaines are good friends. Thomas vouches for you, and that's all I need." She nodded toward the door and Elliot entered.

He settled across from Flynn and Gail, placed a folder on the table, and rested his clasped hands on his opulent belly. "Tell me about your association with Geena Pierce."

Flynn acknowledged the slight nod from Gail and described his relationship with Geena, ending with her breaking their engagement. "She left me July, four years ago, and I haven't seen her since." If necessary, he would provide her recording, but not before he shared it with his lawyer.

Opening the folder, Elliot produced a series of photographs. "Do you recognize these dog tags?"

Flynn leaned in. "They appear to be mine." He swallowed hard. The stains on them had to be blood. Geena's blood. "How...how...?" A nudge from Gail and he said no more.

"Can you explain why your dog tags were found at the crime scene?"

"Don't answer that." Gail said.

"Where were you last Sunday morning, about nine?" The detective raised his sparse, brown eyebrows. His smug expression seemed to indicate Flynn would give him the evidence he needed.

"Is that when Miss Peirce was killed?" the lawyer asked.

Elliot nodded, and she gave Flynn the green light.

Of all days to provide an alibi. Flynn relaxed his shoulders a tad, but the action did nothing to ease the ache in his leg. He described his morning in Jo's hospital room, mentioning Kendall, Ray, and Thomas. He even recalled the name of a nurse. "I left about twelve thirty. Went to my gym. My access card will verify the time. Then I returned home."

"Naturally, we'll verify your alibi." Elliot shoved a legal pad at Flynn. "I need names, addresses, phone numbers."

He jotted down some of the information requested, but without his phone, he couldn't recall numbers. "Thomas Tremaine is my boss. He'll have his daughter's contact information."

The detective stood, picked up the folder and legal pad, and left the room.

Rubbing his thigh, Flynn turned to Gail. "Do you have any idea how long they'll keep me? If I'm going to be here overnight, I'll need my pain meds."

"Let's see what Elliot says when he returns. He might have more evidence. He didn't act as if verifying your alibi would get you off the hook. Is there anything else you need to tell me?"

Flynn glanced at a camera in the corner. "Can they hear us?"

"My previous dealings with this sheriff's department have been all above board. They won't be listening in on our conversation, but if it makes you feel better, whisper."

He described the cryptic message he'd received from Geena, her recording, and the letter she'd hidden in her gym bag.

Gail didn't react to his words. She merely nodded and asked, "Where's the letter and recoding?"

"Jo hid the bag in her storage unit."

"Good. What do you think of Geena's claim about Lewis?"

"I've only met him once, but I trust Geena's opinion of him."

"Could he have killed her?"

Hands fisted under the table, Flynn nodded. "And implicated me by stealing my dog tags. He visited my apartment and must have noticed my military trunk. I only installed a security system later."

"At some point you'll have to share this info with the sheriff. But let's…"

Elliot returned and sat, extracting a couple of sheets of paper from his folder. "Your alibi checks out, Mr. McCaul, however, I'm not convinced you didn't hire someone to kill your ex-fiancée."

"Why would I do that? I have no reason to want her dead."

Gail gave Flynn a disapproving look. "If my client's alibi checks out, then I demand you release him immediately."

"Not so fast. If you're innocent, why'd you book a one-way plane ticket to Ecuador?" He shoved the pages toward Flynn.

Sure enough, it looked like a legit reservation to fly from Seattle to Quito, day after tomorrow. But upon further examination, Flynn sat back, arms crossed. "I did not make that reservation."

"Hold on, let me see." Gail took the pages, scanned them, then frowned at Flynn.

He nudged her. "Give them back to *Detective* Elliot. Check the name, sir."

"I did. Flynn McCaul."

"Right. But notice the spelling of my last name. Whoever made the reservation knows nothing about Scottish names. My McCaul lineage is spelled capital *C* lowercase *a u l*. Not double *l* as in the reservation. A common mistake, but not one I would make."

Elliot reexamined the reservation. "That's, um, not conclusive."

"Yes, it is. My proud Scottish ancestors were insistent on the spelling. And besides, check my computer or phone. I did *not* make that reservation."

"We are checking your laptop, but weren't able to locate your phone."

The longer he sat, the more angry he became. Instead of telling the detective he'd slipped the phone into Jo's bag, he blurted out, "I had no reason to kill Geena. Have you checked out her brother, rather half-brother, Lewis?"

The lines of a frown did little to dent Elliot's fleshy brow. "I didn't know she had a brother."

"Apparently, they weren't close. I didn't know about him either until he visited me a few weeks ago." Flynn glanced at Gail who slowly shook her head.

"What did he want?" Elliot asked.

"He was looking for Geena. I had no information to give him." Ignoring his lawyer's disapproving expression, he added, "I think Lewis stole my dog tags to implicate me. Have you checked them for fingerprints?"

The detective placed the papers in his folder and adjusted his tie.

Gail stood and patted Flynn's shoulder. "If you have nothing else for my client, Detective Elliot, we're leaving. Your evidence is flimsy at best."

"Okay, but, Mr. McCaul, don't leave the area and surrender your passport, please. Um, do you know how to contact Lewis Pierce?"

"I have his business card in my wallet."

"Give it to me when you collect your personal items." Elliot led the way to the desk where Flynn signed for his cane, keys, wallet.

After handing the card to Elliot, Flynn and Gail

were escorted out of the holding area.

"I can give you a lift home." She retrieved keys from her briefcase.

"No thanks, but can I use your phone to call Jo?"

"Of course."

Jo was surprised to get his call, but set out right away.

"I have another appointment, Flynn. Hold onto Geena's recording and letter a bit longer. I'll get back to you when I want you to surrender them to the sheriff."

"Thanks for your help, Gail."

They shook hands, and she drove away in a black Mercedes.

Minutes later, Jo arrived and climbed out of her SUV. Brows knit, mouth in a grim line, she approached him.

Flynn's first instinct was to open his arms wide, but he had to gauge her mood. Was she showing concern because he was almost arrested, or—

Hands on his shoulders, she asked, "Are you all right? How's your leg?" She shook her head. "I was so worried about you." Tears pooled in her eyes.

Then he knew. He slowly drew her to him, wrapping his arms around her waist.

She relaxed, slid her hands up his nape and into his hair. "Flynn, let's go home."

Her breathless voice sent his heart on a merry-go-round ride. Lips inches from hers, he searched her face and leaned closer.

A loud honk interrupted their moment. They were standing in a parking space reserved for a deputy. Flynn sighed and ushed Jo to her vehicle.

Once seated and buckled in, he glanced at her. All business, reversing, pulling out onto the street. Almost as if he imagined the shared lowering of their defenses. He'd take his cue from her and said nothing until she parked in front of his condo. "Thanks for coming out so late to get me. Please come in for a moment."

"Okay."

Although pleased she agreed, her tone told him volumes. She regretted her action.

"Do you want anything to drink?"

She shook her head and sat, poised on the edge of the sofa.

"I'll be back in a minute." He ignored the obvious signs his place had been searched and traipsed to the bathroom to take his pain meds. The angry ants were having a field day scurrying up and down his leg, across his foot, and between his toes. Upon returning to the living room, he removed a couple of magazines from the top of the trunk and opened the lid. "The authorities said they found my dog tags with Geena's body."

Jo gasped. "I'm glad Dad sent Gail to you. I called him after you left and he told me. What else do you know about Geena's murder?"

He sat on the carpet, legs out straight and hiked a

shoulder. "She was found in the woods near here and was apparently killed Sunday morning."

"But you were—"

"Oh, yes, they checked my alibi, and I guess because I'm not in jail, maybe they believe me."

"But your dog tags. Who could have taken them?"

Flynn located a metal lockbox. "I keep them in here. But look, the lock's been forced." He opened the box then tossed it aside exposing his medals. "Lewis came here, remember, and naturally would have noticed my military trunk. Geena broke in to leave me her key, and he could have easily done the same before I installed my security system."

"Do you think he killed Geena?"

"Yes, and I told the sheriff so."

"Good." Jo stood. "I'm going to the office tomorrow. So I need to go home and sleep."

"Is that wise? How's your shoulder and hip? Any headaches?"

She shot him an exasperated look, then smiled. "I'm okay, big brother."

I guess that put me in my place. Just friends. Flynn eased up and shoved his hands into his pockets. "See you tomorrow, then."

A thundering knock at the door. The deputies returned? His heart sank as he opened the door. Flynn blinked. "Ian?"

"I see they let you out of jail."

Words gummed in his throat. He threw his arms

around Ian and pulled him inside. When his brother returned the embrace, Flynn's eyes misted. "How…how did you know?"

The men separated and looked each other up and down.

"Some woman called and made a good case for me to visit."

Flynn turned to Jo. "You?"

She nodded. "I called Melanie first. She couldn't come because Pam is really sick. I took a chance and called Ian. He said he was already in Seattle and would rent a car. I thought that's why you put your phone in my purse."

Flynn laughed. "Not what I had in mind, but thank you."

Ian and Jo greeted each other, exchanging pleasantries.

Overjoyed to see Ian, Flynn shelved his discussion with Jo concerning his actions at the sheriff's department.

At the open door, she turned. "See you."

The smile she gave him warmed his blood. If he'd had two sound feet, he would have kicked his heels together.

VALERIE MASSEY GOREE

Chapter 21

Upon returning to the office after a three-day absence, Jo greeted Brian and Ethan who offered their get well wishes. "Thanks, guys. I'm still achy, but my brain is intact."

"Good to know. While you were gone, I completed the paperwork for the Underwoods' sale. You need to review it." Brian headed to the break room. "Would you like a cup of coffee?"

"Yes, please." She still limited her caffeine intake, but morning coffee was necessary.

Purse stashed in a drawer, Jo eyed the plant Gerry had given her. She shuddered at the memory of his contorted face as he tried to run her down. The plant needed to go. She picked it up and barged into the hall where she bumped into Ethan. Splat. The pot landed on the floor and soil spilled out along with a small, black pebble. "So sorry, Ethan."

"No harm done." He gathered the plant and roots back into the pot.

"I'll get the broom," Brian said.

Jo picked up the pebble and turned it over. Plastic. "What is this thing?"

Ethan set the pot on the counter and took the item from Jo. "It looks like an electronic bug."

"Who's been bugging our office?" Flynn chose that moment to enter the building.

"Gerry. Boyd. The jerk." She returned to her office and slumped into her chair, arms crossed.

Flynn stood at the door. "Obviously, his ploy didn't work. He didn't know where the thumb drive was."

"Right. I never discussed it here. Only at home."

"Well, you don't have to worry about him anymore."

Dunking the device in her coffee cup, she said, "And I won't." *Focus on the positive.* "How's Ian? Did you two stay up all hours?"

Flynn sat and set his briefcase on the floor. "Yes. We had a good, long talk. He's warming up to forgiving me, and I pray our relationship will be back to normal soon." He chuckled then sobered. "Ian said his grudge was also because he liked Geena, but I'd asked her out first. He thought I'd done it on purpose, but I didn't know how he felt."

"And now..." Jo paused. She had no reason to remind Flynn and cleared her throat. "How long is Ian staying?"

"He's due back in Pendleton Sunday evening. Melanie said Pam is on the mend and they are coming over Saturday. Um, would you like to join us?"

The invitation was tempting, but Jo shook her head. "You need to be with your family."

"Okay." He stood and hesitated by the door. "I'd like to meet with you later today."

That sounded ominous. Work or personal? "I don't have much on my calendar." She'd replayed their embrace over and over and wondered how the evening would have ended if they'd been standing on the sidewalk instead of…

"I'll—"

"Hey, bro. Thought I'd come and bug you." Ian's jovial voice sounded from the waiting area.

Jo followed Flynn out of her office. He introduced Ian to Brian and Ethan, then escorted his brother into his office and closed the door.

Seated at her computer, she opened the Underwoods' file and reviewed the documents. Brian had done an excellent job, and now she had to wait on the seller's agent for last minute details. Her phone rang. Why would Flynn call her? "Yes, boss."

"Please come to my office."

Strange request, but she opened his door and sat in the chair beside Ian.

"Don't look so concerned. We're discussing the possibility of Ian purchasing land now with plans to build later when he leaves the Marines."

Jo blew out a breath. She'd imagined the worst. The brothers arguing or on the verge of a fistfight. "How can I help?"

"You know the new developments in the area better than I do. Tell my bro about the ones on the Olympic Peninsula, please."

"Yeah. I don't want to settle anywhere near Seattle."

"Okay." Jo stood and stepped to the map displayed on the wall opposite Flynn's desk. "Come look here. You'll get a better idea of locations, water views, et cetera."

Both men joined her, one on either side. She pointed to different areas as she named potential sites. "Acreage plots are planned here northwest of Sequim. A small development on Marrowstone Island is already advertising. But you might be pleased with a large section of land near Discovery Bay that will be called Diamond Ridge." Jo placed a finger on the spot.

Ian looked closely. "I like that."

"No way, bro. You can't afford land there. Jo, do we have anything available on Cubic Zirconia Ridge?"

Suppressing a giggle, she turned to Ian. "Yes. It is..." she pointed to a tiny island halfway to Canada, "right here."

Ian squinted at the map, then slapped Flynn's shoulder. "Very funny. But you're right. I can't afford much."

"Land will only increase in price. A purchase now will be a good investment." Flynn headed back to his desk.

The brothers kept up a running conversation and

included Jo. Serious, zany, off-the-wall topics interspersed with laughter and somber moments. Jo listened and came to the conclusion the boys must have been a handful growing up.

The revelry was interrupted by Brian knocking and entering the office. "Sorry. Flynn, there are two deputy sheriffs here who need a word."

The smile disappeared from Flynn's face. "Send them in, please. As far as I'm concerned, you two can stay."

Ian and Jo stood and faced the door.

"Mr. McCaul, remember us, Deputies Unger and Lennox? We haven't been able to contact Lewis Pierce. Do you have any other information to share with us? Where does he live? Work? How about a description?"

"I don't know anything about him. I only met him a few weeks ago. He's tall, about—"

"Wait." Jo pulled her phone from her pocket. "I have a picture of him."

"Why?" Flynn asked.

"When he first came to the Gig Harbor office, I heard him discuss you and took a picture, thinking you might need it. But he visited you later." Jo scrolled back weeks and located Lewis's photo. "Here." She passed the phone to Lennox.

"Good. Email this to me, please." She handed Jo a card. "If either of you think of anything else, please let us know."

Before the deputies reached the door, Jo

remembered a vital detail. "He has a son who lives in a group home in Tacoma. Um, sorry I don't recall the name, but ask Brian, our office manager, for Wesley Isenberg's number. His son is there too."

"That's helpful. Thank you." Lennox and Unger left the office, but their visit had acted as a damper.

"I have work to do." Jo looked at Flynn. "Do you still need to talk to me?"

He nodded. "Yeah. Ian and I are going out for lunch. How about this afternoon?"

"Okay." She extended her hand to Ian. "I don't know if I'll see you again, but it's been great meeting you. I'm glad I called and that you and Flynn are no longer at odds. Seriously, when you're in the market for property, give me a call." She beamed at both men. "I'll get you a better deal than anyone else can."

Sauntering from the office, she knew the brothers watched her leave, which set her heart to tingling. Being in the company of two good looking, honest men had lifted her spirits.

The afternoon meeting with Flynn never happened. He was called away to Seattle where he met with a possible financial donor Thomas had arranged last minute. Jo figured she knew what Flynn wanted to discuss, and part of her was glad she didn't have to face him yet. If he brought up their almost kiss, how would she react? Flynn was fast weaving his way into her heart, but she was gun-shy, and although he was nothing like Phil or Max, she still couldn't trust her intuition. He'd have to do a good job convincing her he was the man for her, or she'd quit the job and head south, as far away as possible.

An evening alone, spent evaluating her feelings for Flynn and weighing his numerous positive qualities against his few negative traits, and Jo was ready for their meeting. If he hinted at a relationship with her, she was ready to acknowledge her growing attraction to him.

Upon entering the real estate office the next morning and noting Flynn's closed door, Jo greeted Brian. "Morning, young man. Is Flynn here yet?"

"No. He's off to Poulsbo. The clients he met weeks ago finally agreed on the specs for a house and want to see him today. After that, he has a meeting with Thomas in Gig Harbor about the motel financing. Anything I can do?"

"Thanks, but no." Shoulders sagging, Jo sat at her desk.

Brian appeared at her door with a cup of coffee which he set beside her laptop. "Flynn did say the repairs on Nelda's property are complete and you can list it."

"Great. I'll drive out there this afternoon. I received a call from Nelda yesterday. She wants to sell the place as soon as possible. Too bad we don't have time to stage the whole house, but it won't matter. The magnificent location will catch a buyer's eye."

Jo spent the morning answering email and checking

the paperwork for the Underwoods' sale. Electronic signing allowed buyers and sellers and their agents to complete the necessary documents without meeting face-to-face. By lunchtime, she had all the signatures she needed, and soon would be able to add a hefty commission to her bank account.

On the way to Holly, Jo stopped in Seabeck for a pizza. She took the food with her and ate her lunch on the front deck of Nelda's home. The gardens looked superb, as did the house. She found nothing that needed a touch-up, and after one last walk-through, called Derek, the guy Tremaine Realty used to take drone footage of their properties. He agreed to meet Jo Monday morning.

Aware Flynn would spend Saturday with Ian, Melanie, and her family, Jo made plans to fill her day. First, she visited Kendy in Tacoma. She had reached the point where she didn't think of Robert every time she saw her sister, which was a good sign. Ray had taken Kasi and Blake to the Children's Museum, so Jo was able to discuss her growing attraction to Flynn.

"Dad speaks highly of him, and I like what little I know about him." Kendy refilled Jo's glass of iced tea. "I was impressed with his choice of items he took to you in hospital. He obviously pays attention to your interests. When will you two be able to chat?"

"Maybe tomorrow. Ian returns to base, and I hope to see Flynn at church."

"I will aways be grateful to him for how he helped

you navigate your way back to God."

Jo nodded. "Yeah. If he wants to change careers, I suggest he should become a counselor." She chuckled. "I tease him about it. But seriously, he made me see that by forgiving Mother doesn't mean I have to change who I am." *If she ever tells the truth about your father, I hope you can forgive her too.*

Using her napkin to cover her mouth, Jo clamped her lips together lest her thought became vocal.

"Are you all right?"

"Yes. Just recalling other ways Flynn helped me. He explained why Serena might have been so vindictive. I've also forgiven her, but I don't want to be in her company."

"Good for you, sis. I could use his counsel, too."

"Surely you don't have a problem with forgiveness."

"I do. One of the homeschool parents in our group gets on my nerves. Always demanding we schedule fieldtrips she suggests and do things her way." Kendy rubbed her temples. "She's so annoying. Last week, I challenged her, and she called me all kinds of names. Accused me of sabotaging her efforts and of turning other parents against her. None of which is true."

"You'll do the right thing." Jo was surprised to learn her even-tempered sister lost her cool.

After the light lunch with Kendy, Jo drove to Bradfield Group Home where she'd arranged to meet Wesley and Iris. They sat with Noah in a shaded garden at the rear of the facility.

At first, Noah ignored Jo, but the more she admired the stuffed black bear he held, the more he relaxed. "Hey, Noah, tell me about your new friend."

He shook his head and turned away.

Jo glanced at his parents. "What has he told you about the friend? Do you know his name?"

Rising from the bench, Wesley gestured for her to follow him. They walked a short distance, then he said, "Flynn told me a few things about Lewis, and I've chatted with the man, too. So far, we can't see any problem with Noah and his stepson being friends. However," Wesley sent his son a sideways glance, "we haven't met the boy, uh, man. But Noah sure likes Lewis and his stories about bears." Wesley directed Jo back to the chairs. "Are you aware of something we should know?"

Jo and Flynn might be aware of Lewis's behavior toward Geena, but as yet, they had no solid proof. And since he hadn't been arrested, they didn't know if he was involved in her murder. Jo sat and was surprised when Noah handed her his stuffed bear. "Thank you, Noah. He's so soft." She continued to stroke the bear and said in a low voice, "Do the residents have to be signed out when they leave the facility?" Her conscience demanded she provide a warning.

"Yes." Iris sipped her soda. "Even to come out here with us."

"That's good. I don't want to put a damper on his

friendship with Lewis's stepson, but until Flynn and I have done some research, please tell the staff not to let Noah leave campus with Lewis. He might be involved in criminal activity, and I'm a little concerned that you haven't met his stepson. I don't suppose the staff will provide any details?"

"They won't. We'll keep close tabs on Noah." Iris ruffled her son's hair and he laughed.

Jo stayed a while longer, then headed to her SUV. Her phone buzzed. A call from Mother. Jo opened her door and sat behind the wheel, muscles cavorting in her stomach. Good news or more criticism? "Hello."

Chapter 22

"Joanna, J…Jo."

Jo had never heard her mother's voice so shaky.

"Do you have plans for lunch tomorrow?"

Flynn might ask her out, but she had an inkling Mother's invitation was important. "Not yet."

"Please come home and have a meal with Daddy and me. Just the three of us. At noon."

"Thank you. I'll be there." Jo ended the call as the catch in Mother's voice almost produced tears. Why had she called her Jo? What did Mom want?

Driving back to Silverdale where Jo had a dinner date with her cycle club members, she dwelt on her mother's possible motives, but when she parked outside the restaurant, she still had no clear idea. *Stop speculating. Just go and keep a positive attitude. And don't stir the pot.*

Danny, Emma, and Vic sat at a table, scanning the menus. Jo joined them and was greeted with a chorus of well wishes and questions.

"You're looking good."

"How's the shoulder?"

"Can you ride with us next Saturday?"

After the meal, they played foosball until late. They were good company for Jo, and she went home tired, but ready for meeting Mother.

Although the church service was uplifting, Jo was disappointed Flynn wasn't there. He was probably still with Ian and Melanie, maybe taking Ian to the airport. She had wanted moral support from him before she set out for her luncheon, but instead, she drove to her parents' home with a prayer playing over and over on her lips. "Please, Father God, guide my tongue and give me a spirit of peace."

Dad answered the door and took Jo out to the shaded patio. Mom sat at the table, but stood as Jo approached, hands extended.

Jo clasped her hands then sat, staring at her mother, not sure her eyes were focusing. Mother wore no makeup, and her hair touched her shoulders. Jo couldn't remember the last time she'd seen the woman's unadorned face or her hair down, loose and free, or her fingernails without their signature pink polish. Even in this natural state, Mother was beautiful. Yet, Jo sensed an underlying vulnerability.

Jo chose to wear a dress she'd kept from her business days. A designer number in salmon pick with a spray of greenery from the hem up her left side to the waist which was cinched with a wide brown belt to match her brown heels. She wasn't sure if she dressed to impress Flynn or Mother. Probably Mother. On this occasion, Jo felt overdressed as Mother wore a white cotton pant suit, uncharacteristically not tailored or fashioned from expensive fabric.

Throughout the simple meal of chicken salad and crispy rolls, her parents kept up a genial conversation. No criticism, no second guessing. Mother asked after Jo's health, her shoulder, hip, and bump on the head. Jo answered in short sentences, still not sure if she'd fallen down a rabbit hole and would soon meet Alice or the Madhatter.

After Dad removed their plates and set out bowls of chocolate ice cream—Jo's favorite—she was ready to question the whole surreal scenario.

But Mother set aside her unfinished bowl and cleared her throat. "Jo, dear. I asked you here today to apologize again, and to tell you that I am deeply mortified by how I've treated you for years." She held up a hand to Jo when she began to protest. "Let me finish, child. I don't deserve your forgiveness, but I crave it." Mother lowered her head and Dad passed her a tissue. After wiping her eyes, she continued. "When we were on vacation in Victoria, I spent hours walking along the beach and reviewing my treatment of you. I have no excuses and I admit I was a hypocrite and behaved badly toward you. I prayed for guidance."

Dad said, "You're doing well, Anita, darling."

Mother drew in a breath and took Jo's hand. "Can we start afresh, you and me, mother and daughter?"

Throat thick with emotion, Jo nodded and squeaked out, "I'd like that."

"I am proud of you, from the first race you won—I have your photo holding the trophy on my dresser—to the fabulous job you're doing in Tremaine Realty. I'm not expecting an instant bond between us, but all I want is for you to agree that we can begin again."

Jo nodded, tears ready to seep out of her eyes. She accepted a tissue from Dad and swiped at her cheeks. His eyes were moist, too. Some vacation they'd had.

Mother released Jo's hand and ran her fingers through her silver hair. "I have more to share. I won't try to make you into another Kendall. I accept you as you are, with different opinions and viewpoints. I've been very selfish, trying to make you more like your sister. She and I agree on so many things, but you were always the independent thinker, and I couldn't understand that."

The sincerity in Mother's voice touched Jo's heart. She relaxed against the chair, hands clasped in her lap.

"By the way, you look lovely. The colors you choose suit you, and I can't believe I tried to change your selection. You discovered what suited you a long time ago." She chuckled. "I remember shopping with you as a young girl and you didn't like my choices, and then we'd argue. But I won't rehash events that must have been painful for you." She wiped her eyes. "I'm almost done. Ever since your accident and describing your miscarriage, I've noticed a change in you. You're softer, not as combative, or argumentative. You must have been carrying a heavy burden which you obviously didn't want to share with us, and again, I apologize for being the type of person, the type of mother you felt you couldn't unburden yourself to. That's on me. I love you, Jo. And one more thing, I promise to never shove another eligible man at you." A sweet smiled graced her face.

Before Jo could respond, Dad took his turn to clear his throat. "Punkin, your mother and I want to tell Kendall about her father, and we'd like you to be present. Can you do that for us?"

Now the tears fell. Jo stood, upending her chair. Her parents rose too, and Jo slipped her arms around them. Mother's hold tightened, and Jo relished the tender moment, a genuine embrace, not just a formality. *Thank You, God, for Your grace and forgiveness.*

Chapter 23

With Ian back at Pendleton, and Melanie and family home in Seattle, Flynn dressed to face a new week at the office. He'd cherished time spent with his siblings, especially renewing the relationship with Ian. Now, to address another relationship. With Jo. No need to be coy or tiptoe around the subject. He called her and asked her to meet him at the park near the Silverdale office.

On the way to the park, he stopped at a food truck and bought two large cups of coffee and two muffins. Fortified by the caffeine and sweet blueberry bites, he waited, glancing up at every vehicle which drove by.

Jo arrived a few minutes later. She looked stunning. An emerald, green top which set off her vibrant red curls and matched her eyes and made them sparkle, and a cream-colored skirt. The first time she hadn't worn slacks and boots to the office. He stood, removed his jacket, and spread it out on the wooden bench opposite. "Don't want your skirt to get dirty."

"Thank you, kind sir." She sat and gave him a

brilliant smile. Obviously, she'd left her purse in the car, and she set her keys on the table.

"I hope you like muffins."

She removed the chocolate chip delicacy and then sipped the coffee. "Thanks. Did you have a good time with your family?"

"I did. Ian and I are on a sound footing and I made plans to visit him later in the year. How was your weekend? You look…content." He knew he was delaying the reason he'd asked her to the park, but he needed time to build up his courage.

"I have two things to share, one interesting, the other very important. I stopped by the group home in Tacoma and spent time with Noah and his parents. Wesley still has not met Lewis's stepson, and Noah wouldn't even tell me his name. I advised them not to let Noah leave the facility with Lewis. I didn't know what else to tell them. Have you heard anything from the sheriff concerning Lewis?"

"I haven't. You did the right thing. I hope we are mistaken about Lewis. Now, tell me your other news."

"I had a lovely, and I mean lovely lunch with my folks yesterday. Mother apologized again, and this time I know she's sincere. She admitted to trying to mold me in Kendy's image, and has finally realized that's impossible and not her job. My folks plan to tell Kendall about Robert and want me to be present. I consider that an honor." Jo huffed out a deep breath. "Mother and I are on a sound footing, too."

Flynn nodded, dusted crumbs off his shirt, set his elbows on the table, and looked at Jo. "Praise God, you and Anita have healed the gap, Ian and I are friends again, and you agreed to meet me here this morning." He jutted his chin toward the water. "I chose this beautiful setting away from our co-workers for a good reason."

Setting aside her coffee cup and half-eaten muffin, she tilted her head. "And what is that reason, Mr. McCaul?"

"I'll get straight to the point. I don't want to ruin our friendship, but I'd like to build on that relationship. Maybe you've noticed, I really like you, enjoy your company. What do you think?" He held his breath until he needed oxygen. His heartbeat increased and beads of sweat tickled his upper lip. He swiped them away.

Jo frowned and scrunched up a paper napkin. "I like you too, more so after your stint at the sheriff's department. You're more approachable, dare I say more humble, and those qualities are very admirable."

"Thanks. I'm trying."

"But I have such a poor track record with boyfriends. I often wonder if I'm the problem and that's why guys run from me or try to control me."

"Hold on. You are not the problem. Some men don't like strong women, and maybe when a relationship gets serious you back away because you don't want to get hurt again. We can proceed slowly, as long as you don't make me wait too long. I'd say…two weeks is long enough." He returned her smile. "Remember, I've been hurt, too, but I've changed my mind about deserving happiness. Ian helped me jump over that hurdle."

"Good."

He reached for her hands and held tight. "So, we have a deal. Take it slowly, see what develops. Spend more time together outside the office."

She giggled. "I feel like a teenager, all tingly inside." A rosy blush infused her cheeks.

Releasing her hands, he eased out from the bench, gathered her muffin into the sack, and tossed the empty cups into a trash bin.

Jo carefully stepped over the bench and handed him his jacket. "Very considerate of you."

"Thanks. I suppose we should go to work."

"Agree. I'm meeting Derek, the drone guy, at Nelda's property later this morning."

"That's such a magnificent house. It won't be on the market long." He stepped on an exposed root, throwing himself off balance. Vanity had made him leave his cane in the truck. He reached out and connected with Jo's arm. She immediately steadied him, her face inches from his. "I'm glad you were next to me." A minty scent wafted up, but he ignored it and focused on her parted lips. Dare he? Yes. He slipped his arms around her. She didn't resist and slid her hands up his chest toward his neck.

"Maybe I made a mistake. Two weeks is—"

"Too long to wait." She drew his head down and brushed her soft, warm lips over his, tentatively at first.

He groaned and surrendered to the kiss, but she pushed away when two teens rode by and whistled and hollered.

A toss of her curls and she grabbed his hand, pulling him toward the car park. "Work, then play." She climbed into her SUV and drove away without a backward glance, but not before Flynn noticed her beaming smile.

He sat in his truck and set the sack on the passenger seat. *Well that went better than he dreamed possible.* "Thank You, God."

~

Flynn couldn't concentrate on the list of financial donors he needed to thank. Whenever he tried to focus on a personal letter, Jo's playful smile filled his mind and heart. She'd left for Nelda's place, but not before she agreed to meet him for supper. He'd already booked a table at a new Mediterranean restaurant in Bremerton, and he counted down the hours.

When Jo phoned him close to noon, he leaned back in his chair and conjured up her beautiful face. "Did you—" He'd almost said, *Did you miss me already?* but bit his tongue before the arrogant words slipped out. "Did you complete the drone footage?"

"Yes. Derek will upload it to our website later today, and then we can list the property. He sent the drone through the house, into every room, and of course it soared over the property, taking in the sunlight glinted off the water. I'm excited to have been part of the restoration, from messed up to beautiful."

"You're good at that. Will you be back soon?"

"Unfortunately, no. Eileen Trask, our property management assistant, needs me to check on a rental where neighbors report strange goings-on. Not sure what I'll find. So, looks like I won't see you until this evening."

"I can't wait. Bye." He wanted to add *darling*, or *sweetheart*, but wasn't sure how Jo would react to the popular endearments. Aha. He'd have to invent one, just for her. One to match her personality. Of course, he could use *querida*, Spanish for sweetheart, but axed the idea. He recalled the conversation about her father not agreeing to the name her mother had chosen. Candy. Candy cane in honor of her red hair. Nope. Too juvenile. He gave himself a mental shove. Any term with a special meaning had to be spontaneous, not manufactured.

Pleased with his resolution, he set about writing the letters.

As the sun sank behind the mountains, Flynn waited outside the restaurant, please he wore the only suit he possessed. Jo arrived and he met her as she climbed out of her SUV. She'd changed out of her skirt and top, and now wore a sleek black dress with thin straps. He took her arm and kissed her on the cheek, sure she didn't want her lipstick smeared. "You look marvelous."

"Thanks. So do you." She squeezed his forearm.

During the meal of moussaka, their conversation centered around getting to know each other. No business, no discussion about forgiveness, just sharing fun details about childhood memories and dreams for the future.

"Once I've repaid my folks for bailing me out, I had thought about getting back into interior design." Jo sipped her iced tea. "But I'm rethinking my choices."

"You're not interested in staying in real estate?"

"No. I like this business of raising money for worthy causes. I really enjoyed helping you."

"You'd be good at the job. I'll give you a glowing reference."

She smiled, then laughed. But the idea seemed to sink in.

"You have a presence."

"Um, what do you mean?"

"When you enter a room, people take notice. Did you see how almost every person watched as you walked across the restaurant to our table?"

She shook her head.

"And not just because of your height and beautiful red hair. You carry yourself with confidence which projects trustworthiness and sincerity."

"Come on, Flynn. Be serious." Although she negated his praise, her cheeks glowed with a rosy blush.

"I am. Combined with your organizational skills and job sequence analysis, displayed in documental repairs needed on Nelda's home, you're a perfect candidate for fund raising."

She fanned her face. "A job like that would require lots of traveling."

The waiter stopped by and asked if anyone wanted dessert.

Flynn was glad when Jo declined as he was ready to have a private moment with her. He accepted the bill and placed his credit card in the folder then took Jo's hand. "I've enjoyed our evening together. Next time, I'll pick you up so I can take you home. No sense bringing two vehicles."

"Okay, but don't feel we have to eat out all the time. I can cook."

"So can I. Okay, we'll play it by ear." The waiter returned his card and he signed the receipt. "Are you ready?"

She stood and picked up her small purse, and he placed his hand in the small of her back as they left the restaurant. They stopped at her car which she'd parked toward the back of the lot.

He slid his arms around her waist and drew her closer. She placed her hands on his shoulders and leaned in. Covering her lips with his, he kissed her until they were both breathless.

"This isn't exactly taking it slow." Jo ran her hand across his nape and into his hair.

"I've waited a long time for the perfect woman to come into my life. As far as I'm concerned, you're the one for me."

Her gaze seemed to search his eyes. Why hadn't she responded to his declaration? Had he been too forthcoming? "You don't—"

She placed a finger on his lips. "Hush and kiss me again."

Chapter 24

Working in close proximity to Flynn added to Jo's contentment. Sure, they discussed business, but they also shared quiet moments together. She was almost ready to tell him he was her chosen mate, too.

After receiving the hefty commission from the Underwoods' sale, Jo knocked on Flynn's open door, checkbook in hand. "I have something for you." She could hardly concentrate on anything but his face. He wore a blue shirt which set off his blond hair and deepened the gray of his eyes. His smile set her heart to tumbling and weakened her knees. She sat and blew out a breath.

"To what do I owe this honor?" He rocked in his chair and kept his gaze on her.

"I want to donate to the fund for the motel."

He stilled his chair and leaned on the desk. "I just had a long chat with Thomas. He suggested I form a not-for-profit foundation because I hope this is the first of many properties I can turn into housing for veterans."

"That's a great idea."

"Yeah. It will take time, so for now, checks are welcome. Thanks for helping me set up a local bank account."

Jo handed over the check. "Not as much as I'd like to give you, but I want the rest of my commission to pay off my parents. My debt to them has been whittled down, sale by sale. I'll be free with one more similar to the Underwoods'."

"You're forgetting one important fact. Won't you receive commission from the sale of Nelda's place?"

Springing out of her chair, Jo twirled and twirled until she stopped bedside Flynn. He pulled her into his lap, and she latched her arms around his neck. "How could I forget Nelda? We've been working on her property forever." Jo kissed Flynn and stood. "I have one last transaction then I'm going to Gig Harbor. I want to confirm the asking price for her place with Dad. I'll probably be late home." At the door she stopped and said over her shoulder, "I was going to attend your self-defense class this evening. Maybe next week. See you tomorrow."

Although Jo could have conducted her business with Dad over the phone, she wanted to see him and Mother. Just to make sure she hadn't dreamt the events from last Sunday. Their meeting at his office was everything Jo could have wanted. Delight at seeing her, no criticism of her clothing, and congratulations on a job well done with Nelda's property. Dad set the sale price well above what Jo had anticipated.

She drove home with a joy-filled heart. Relationship with Mother on the way to being repaired, baby steps along her walk of faith, and a man she cared for deeply who seemed to be in love with her.

While at her desk the next day, Flynn hollered from his office, "Jo, come here. Quickly."

She hurried the few steps to his door where Brian already stood. They entered the office and Flynn motioned for them to look at his phone. "A text from Lewis and this photo."

Jo took the phone. "Noah. Bound and gagged. Look at his eyes. He must be so scared." Her heart sank and she chewed her bottom lip.

"Do you want me to call the sheriff?" Brian asked.

"No, thanks. Jo and I need to sort this out." Flynn sat in one of the chairs in front of his desk and Jo settled in the other.

"Let me know if you change your mind." Brian discreetly left the office and closed the door.

"I will. Read the text, please, Jo."

"'If you want to see him alive, bring me Geena's letter. The one she gave to you for safekeeping. I'll provide directions in one hour. And don't contact the authorities. I'm watching you.'" Hand trembling, she held the phone and studied the screen. "What are you going to do?"

"I guess comply with his demands. We can copy the letter in Geena's journal, use gloves to handle it."

Meanwhile, Jo enlarged the photo of Noah and checked his surroundings. "Wait. I know where Noah is. At least where this photo was taken. I've been riding out there many times. I can go—"

"Not by yourself. I'll come with you."

"We need to ride part of the way."

"That's okay. You have two bikes, right?"

She nodded. Maybe they could rescue Noah before Wesley and Iris found out. "If Lewis is watching, he might think we're going to retrieve the journal." She snickered. "Actually, Geena's gym bag is in my storage unit with my bikes."

"Get the journal while we're there. Just in case."

Jo drove to the unit, keeping watch for any tail, but saw no suspicious vehicles. "I don't think he followed us."

"I was checking, too."

She opened the door and handed Flynn a hand pump. "Check the tires, please." Helmets in hand, Jo located Geena's bag and removed the journal.

After adding air to the tires, Flynn stashed the book in his pocket.

"I'm glad I'm wearing pants and boots today. Let's load up the bikes and be on our way."

With both bikes secured in the rack on Jo's SUV, she drove to Mission Creek Trailhead, southwest of Bremerton, not too far away.

"How do you know where the photo was taken?"

"We've ridden here many times and I also like to

come by myself. It's an easy ride. Most of the trail is through woodlands except for one section where the path is eroding along a cliff. The trail has been rerouted, but I recognized the old section. There's a narrow ledge below the path. That's where Noah is. Or was."

While she talked, Flynn pulled off his shoe and unstrapped the black contraption from his foot and calf. He adjusted his sock, then put his shoe back on. "Sorry, I had to remove my brace. It hinders my movements as I discovered when I rode with my nieces." He tucked his pant legs into his socks.

Good move. To keep the fabric from getting caught in the spokes.

"Now you can keep up with me." She noted he systematically clenched his fists, then wiped his palms on his thighs, as if anxious.

Before she could inquire, he placed his hand on her shoulder. "I have to pray, Jo. Father, please keep Noah safe and help us find him before Lewis shows up. In Jesus' name. Amen."

"Thank you. We're here." She screeched to a halt and parked. Once out of the vehicle, she handed Flynn a helmet. "The track's going to be messy since we had rain last night. Please be careful." She snapped her helmet and climbed on her bike. "This way."

The first part of the trail cut through thick forest with more small rocks and twigs than Jo remembered. She glanced back to check on Flynn. He managed to keep behind her, although his mouth formed a grim line in his set jaw.

Ten minutes later, she stopped at the closed section, raised the chain and pushed her way under. Flynn did the same. She motioned him close and whispered, "Lewis might be nearby. Obviously, this is the hazardous part. Keep away from the edge, and if the path gets any narrower, we'll have to walk."

He nodded and proceeded behind her.

Sure enough, the path became dangerously narrow. She balanced her bike against a tree, removed her helmet, and pointed forward. "A few more yards."

Their footsteps were cushioned by years of fallen leaves and pine needles. In the distance, a soft voice mingled with the sound of a breeze stirring in the branches above them. Jo turned and Flynn nodded. He'd heard it too.

Footprints in the mud at the edge of the path marked the spot she remembered. Grasping Flynn's hand, she leaned over and quickly drew back. "Noah's down there, on his side. He might be asleep, but he's no longer bound or gagged." She slapped her thigh. "Since I knew about this ledge, I should have brought rope."

"Don't fret. At least we found him. You found him." Flynn unbuckled his belt. "Hold onto this and I'll lower you down."

"Okay." Jo sat on the verge and wound the belt around her right wrist. "Good thing it's so long."

"Hey." He grinned, lay on his stomach, and wound the other end around his wrist. "Ready?"

She sucked in a breath and eased herself over the edge, grabbing onto exposed roots to aid her decent. Soft mud covered her clothing as Flynn let her down inch by inch. Almost there, then Noah woke up. She should have alerted him to her presence, but she was too concerned with getting her feet on solid rock.

Noah took one look at Jo and got to his feet, lashing out and screaming, "Go away. You'll scare the bears." He caught her leg and yanked. "You're a bad person."

Jo lost her grip on the mud-smeared belt. She fell on her left side, and as she gazed up at Flynn, all she could think was how much her shoulder hurt and how her head ached. A deep, black void swallowed her.

Chapter 25

"No! Jo, Jo? Are you all right?" Blood thundering in his brain, Flynn stared at the still form of his beloved on the rocks below.

Noah stood on the narrow ledge with his hands on his hips, mumbling something about bears. At least he wasn't injured.

Flynn called again, "Jo. Wake up." But she didn't stir. He sat and fished his phone from his muddy pants. No signal. To be expected midst the thick forest, but he dared not go in search of a clearing. He had no idea why Noah attacked Jo and couldn't risk leaving them together while Jo was unconscious. And the threat Lewis might be in the vicinity hovered over him.

"Jo, my love. Please respond." Flynn looked at Noah who held his hands over his ears. "Noah, I'm friends with your dad and I need your help."

"I don't know you. You're making too much noise. All this commotion is going to scare the bears."

A clue as to how Lewis tricked Noah into accompanying him. "But you do know Joanna

Tremaine. She might be hurt. Can you try to wake her, please?"

He seemed to contemplate Flynn's request, then knelt beside Jo and shook her arm. "Jo, wake up. The bears will be coming soon." Next, he picked up a dead leaf and brushed it over her cheeks, lips, nose.

A smart move. The tickling was enough to rouse her. She brushed the leaf away, turned her head and moaned. "What...? Oh." She looked up at Flynn then at Noah.

"Jo, do you have any broken bones? Take a careful assessment before you move."

She bent her legs, patted her left shoulder. "No, but I aggravated past injuries."

Flynn exhaled a big breath. "Noah, please help Jo to sit."

"Okay, but then will you both stop talking?" He grabbed Jo's extended hand and pulled her to a sitting position.

"Don't stand, yet, Jo. I'm going to walk down the trail until I can make a phone all."

"We'll be fine, won't we Noah? Tell me about the bears."

But Flynn didn't have to go far. A few yards along the trail, he held up his phone again and this time got a signal. He called the sheriff's department and explained his predicament.

"The young man with you is Noah Isenberg?"
"Yes."

"Great. There's a Purple Alert out on him."

"A what?" Noah's raised voice concerned Flynn and he slowly walked back to the cliff, careful to keep within range of the signal.

"Purple is used for adults who are not senior citizens. His parents notified authorities. Is he all right?"

"Physically, yes, but he's becoming agitated, and I fear for Jo's safety."

"We'll be there as soon as we can and we'll bring ATVs to transport Jo, and Noah, if necessary."

Flynn returned to the cliff, settled on his stomach and studied the situation. Jo still sat, resting her head on her bent knees. Noah paced the confined space, muttering about bears.

"Hey, Jo. I called the sheriff. Help is on the way. Noah was reported missing, so I'm sure his folks will arrive soon."

She didn't move her head, but said, "You should get Noah off this ledge. He's threatening to jump and is accusing me of spoiling Lewis's plans."

How could he pull Noah out, and then Jo? His belt would be of no use now, but a chain would. He hurried back to the main trail, and using brute strength, removed the chain from the two metal posts. In his haste to return, he tripped and almost landed flat on his face, but he gained his balance just in time and ran to the edge. On his stomach in the mud again, he lowered the chain. "Jo, please help wrap the chain around

Noah's waist and show him how to hold onto one end."

Flynn watched Jo do as he requested, the whole time reassuring the young man that this was the culmination of his big adventure. "The bears won't come down here. You have to be up there with Flynn to see any animals." She was a natural. Although Noah wasn't a child, she knew the right things to say.

Noah stood and squinted up at Flynn. "I'm ready. Are you strong enough to pull me up?"

"I am." All the weightlifting in the gym was about to pay off. "As I pull, pretend you're walking up a wall. Okay?"

"Yes."

Flynn pulled hand over hand, and within fifteen seconds, Noah was next to him on the trail. "Good job. Now let's give Jo the chain."

"That was fun. Can we do it again?"

"Sure, just not today. Please sit on that log while I help Jo." Flynn lowered the chain. "Wrap this around your waist."

"I will, but I can only hold on with one hand. My left shoulder is on fire, and I don't know about walking up the side. My hip is painful, too, and my head throbs. I probably have another concussion."

"Of course. I wasn't thinking. What are our options?" The chain was at least twelve feet long. "I have an idea. Wrap the middle of the chain around your waist, then toss the other end to me. I'll hold both ends. That way you only have to hold on with your right hand. I'll do all the work. You concentrate on not injuring yourself."

"Okay. I'll try." She had to toss the free end of the chain to him several times before he could grab it.

"Ready? Here goes." He braced his feet on an exposed tree root and pulled with every ounce of power he could muster, a prayer on his lips the whole time. He might have a shriveled leg, but he was thankful for his upper body strength at this moment.

Muddy, breathless, Jo was finally beside him. He unwrapped the chain, scooted back from the edge, and took her in his arms, ignoring the screams from his shoulder and back muscles. "Thank, you Lord."

Noah joined them and patted Jo's shoulder. "I'm glad you're safe. Sorry I pulled your leg."

She whispered, "No problem, Noah. Your parents are coming to see you." Looking up at Flynn, she added, "Thank you for saving us."

His heart beat thumped in his ears, from the recent exertion, from holding Jo, and from being her hero. He smiled and brushed her hair off her mud-streaked forehead.

"Are you husband and wife?" Noah asked.

Jo snuggled against Flynn's chest then raised her head. "Why would you think that?"

"Because you look at each other the same way my mom and dad do."

Flynn chuckled. "From the mouths of babes—"

"Hey, Mr. Lewis. You came. Where are the bears?"

Noah jumped up and ran down the trail.

Flynn and Jo turned in time to see Lewis hug Noah.

"Hello, my friends. Did you bring what I require?" He carried a coil of rope over his shoulder and when he opened his jacket, a handgun rested in his waistband.

"Yes. No need to get violent, Lewis." Flynn latched onto a nearby branch and hauled himself upright.

Noah tugged on Lewis's sleeve. "I'm still waiting for the bears."

He shoved the young man aside. "Don't do that again. I'll tell you where they are later. Now, Flynn. where's the journal?"

The look of disappointment on Noah's face tugged at Flynn's sanity. He clenched his teeth and fisted his hands. *Come one step closer, Lewis, and you'll regret ever entering my life.*

Jo's question saved him from committing a crime. She had moved away from the edge. "Hey, Lewis, tell us about Geena. We're curious. Did you kill her?"

The man smirked. "Of course, I did. She inherited all the money, and I needed it. Don't you think I was clever to steal your dog tags, Flynn? And since we're being so honest, there was no box of items from a neighbor or diary from Geena either."

"What about the lawyer's death?" Flynn said the words through clenched teeth.

"How do you...? Never mind. There was no lawyer, of course." He approached Jo and reached for his gun.

Not to be hushed so easily, Noah stepped in front of

Lewis. "You promised. I don't like it when people break their promises."

Seizing Noah, Lewis wrapped the rope around and around his torso, all the while getting closer to the cliff.

Flynn met Jo's gaze. They seemed to read each other's minds. She eased up and grabbed Noah's arm just as he slipped in the mud at the edge and yanked him to safety.

Lewis released the rope then pulled his gun and aimed first at Jo then at Flynn.

Flynn called out, "Here's Geena's journal." He tossed the book at Lewis, distracting him long enough for Flynn to rush and overpower him. The man was no match for his anger-fueled strength. Subdued with his hands held in a vise grip, Lewis struggled, and Flynn hollered, "Jo, bring me the rope, please."

Later, with Lewis securely tied up and Noah sulking on a log a few feet away, Flynn cradled Jo in his arms while sitting in the mud. They were safe, unharmed, and he had accomplished the recuse without succumbing to a panic attack. In fact, since praying in the car, he hadn't lost control for a second. He sighed and tightened his hold on Jo.

However, their moment of peace was broken when persistent Noah asked again, "When will I see the bears?"

Jo chucked against Flynn's chest. "Ask your parents to take you to Woodland Park Zoo in Seattle. They have lots of bears."

"Oh, yes. I remember. We've been there before. Cool."

That seemed to pacify Noah. He paced the trail, gathering twigs which he dumped at Lewis's feet.

"He's an interesting person. And very perceptive. Do you remember what he said about us?" Flynn kissed Jo's temple.

She nodded.

"I think we should validate his notion." He looked up through the foliage to patches of blue sky. *Bless my words, dear Father, God.* Filled with courage, he said, "Jo, I love you. You are my beloved, my belle. I want you in my forever life. Will you marry me?"

"My belle? I like that. Yes, Errol Flynn McCaul, I will marry you."

He ran his hand through her mussy curls, trailed a finger down her cheek to her lips.

She shuddered and gasped.

He traced the outline of her lips and she sighed. Then he covered her quivering lips with his.

"Hey, I hear engines. ATVs, if I'm not mistaken. Do you know what they are? All-Terrain-Vehicles. Must be the sheriff coming to take me to see the bears."

Flynn and Jo broke apart and laughed.

Noah had the last word.

THE END

Bio:

Award winner Valerie Massey Goree resides in the beautiful Hill Country, northwest of San Antonio.

After serving as missionaries in her home country of Zimbabwe and raising two children, Valerie and her husband, Glenn, a native Texan, moved to Texas. She worked in the public school system for many years, focusing on students with special needs. Now retired, Valerie spends her time writing, traveling, and spoiling her grandchildren.

Valerie loves to hear from her readers.

Check Valerie's website to learn more about her romantic suspense novels and Glenn's non-fiction books:
www.valeriegoreeauthor.com

Dear Reader:

Heroines come in all shapes and sizes. Many of my heroines are not dainty and ultra-feminine. I hope you enjoyed getting to know Jo and leaning how she comes to accept her physical attributes. Halfway through writing *Every Hidden Thing*, I moved to a new apartment. My neighbor, now in her eighties, silver-haired, and stooped, was a redhead most of her life and close to six feet tall. When I described my heroine to her, she was tickled that someone actual wrote about a woman who resembled her.

As Jo states, we are all unique children of God. We might not be in control of what we look like on the outside, but we can definitely change our inner attributes.

I love connecting with my readers.

Sign up for my monthly newsletter:
https://bit.ly/VGJoinMyCommunity

Check out my Facebook author page.
www.facebook.com/ValerieMasseyGoree
Visit my website: www.valeriegoreeauthor.com
My books are also featured at:
www.goodreads.com/search? and
https://www.bookbub.com/search?

Sincerely,

Valerie Massey Goree

274

Valerie's next project is a trilogy. Peril in Triplicate tells the stories of three sisters. Here is a sneak peek at Book 1, *Jan's Justice.*

ONE

Determined to handle the anniversary of her fiancé's disappearance like any other day, Jan Sullivan hauled her backpack to a wooden bench in Canfield Park. She had one goal this afternoon—to complete the commissioned sketches for a children's book. With pad on her lap and her favorite Faber-Castell graphite pencil in hand, she studied the raucous activity of children on the playground equipment. Situated in a family neighborhood on the north side of San Antonio, the park provided her with ideal models enjoying the sunny Saturday.

A nearby toddler's giggle brought a smile to Jan's face. She hadn't felt this content for a long time and puffed out a sigh. Months ago, she'd realized January 14 was just a date on the calendar and she'd stopped blaming herself for Bradly's disappearance. If he suddenly returned to her life, she'd be relieved, but she wouldn't marry him. She couldn't pinpoint the exact reason, except maybe she never loved him enough. And, truth be told, maybe that's why he left—he didn't want to marry her, either.

As she set pencil to parchment, her phone chirped. Sliding it out of her jacket pocket, she noted no name appeared with the number. Nothing unusual in that. She often received unsolicited business calls.

"Jan Sullivan speaking."

"Afternoon, Ms. Sullivan." The gruffness of the man's voice sounded muffled and unfamiliar. "Where is Bradley Buchanan?"

Surely she hadn't heard correctly. "Excuse me?"

"Don't be coy. Where's Bradley?"

A gust of wintry air forced icy tentacles through her jacket to stab her heart. Bradley Buchanan, her fiancé.

In spite of her earlier *joie de vivre*, painful memories of his unexplained abandonment resurfaced. She clutched the sketchpad to her chest. "I don't know."

"It's January 14. Aren't you thinking about him today?

The caller knew when Bradley disappeared.

Contentment oozed away as her heart rate ratcheted up a notch. Blood tha-thumped in her head. "Who are you? Why do you need to know where he is?"

"Doesn't matter who I am." His words dripped with anger. "I won't leave you alone until I get what I want." He paused for a couple of seconds. "I know where you live."

A sharp click severed the call. Jan stared at the phone while a shudder snaked along her shoulders.

Obviously the man wanted something besides Bradley's whereabouts. Rattled but still in control, she scrolled to *calls received* and hit *send* on the most recent. It rang and rang but no one answered.

She shoved her phone back into her pocket and glared at her blank sketchpad. So much for her plan. Even though perfect subjects surrounded her, the mysterious phone call numbed her fingers and gave life to a seed of fear. Why did the caller think she knew anything about Bradley's disappearance? Recalling the underlying threat in his words, the thumping in her head increased. Her efforts to keep her past from intruding on her present had failed.

A troop of little girls climbed onto the swings in front of her. Their squeals of joy reminded Jan of her reason for being at the park. Inhaling cool air into her lungs, she resolved she wouldn't allow a phone call to control her actions. She squared her shoulders and set to work.

Focused on the laughing kids, she produced pages of detailed sketches. With each pencil swirl, the heavy mood lifted as light crept into the dark corners of her soul. Bradley and the conjured up man asking about him became faint silhouettes.

After studying one picture, Jan added more detail to the flying tresses of the girl, then tilted her head. A small smile of satisfaction crept onto her lips. She nodded once. "That's it."

In a fluid motion, she turned to a clean page and

outlined another child.

"Sarah! Watch where you're going!"

Jan raised her head at the masculine yell.

Heedless of the warning, a little three- or four-year-old girl raced toward the swings on the path to an inevitable collision.

Tossing aside her sketchpad, Jan lurched forward and snatched up the child. "Whew, that was close." She set the girl down on the grass and placed her hands on the tot's tiny shoulders. "Are you okay?"

Huge blue eyes dominated the scared little face.

Before the child could answer, a man rushed over and repeated the question. "Sarah, are you all right?" He fell to his knees in front of her.

"Daddy, why are you yelling? Why did she grab me?" The child's wide-eyed stare flew from her father's face to Jan.

"Honey, this lady saved you from getting hit. You weren't looking where you were going."

She wrapped her arms around his neck as he picked her up and stood. Smiling, he turned to Jan. "Thank you."

"Glad I got to her in time."

"I'm grateful for your quick action." He kissed his daughter's cheek and extended his hand.

Its warmth surprised Jan. She raised her gaze to his face and took in his dark brown hair and blue eyes, the color of his daughter's, before he withdrew his hand.

"Thanks again." He inclined his head and carried

Sarah to the opposite side of the playground.

Jan returned to the bench to retrieve her sketchpad and pencil which had fallen onto the pea gravel. Dirt smudges covered the page she'd been working on. She tore it out, sat down, and stared at the clean sheet. The incident with the man and his daughter derailed her concentration. Even with the deadline looming, how could she sketch now?

After setting the pencil behind her ear, Jan squeezed her hands together. Warmth the man's hand had generated lingered. A little butterfly somersaulted in her stomach. What blue eyes he had. They reminded her of the Mediterranean Sea. It had been a long time since she'd noticed a man's eyes. It had been a long time since she'd noticed a man, period.

Removing the pencil, Jan nibbled its end. If she was going to notice men again, maybe she shouldn't begin with a guy who was probably married. She shook her head but her mental image of the dimple hovering at the corner of his mouth and the afternoon stubble scattered on his firm jaw refused to budge.

While she studied the last sketch she'd done, Sarah and her father paraded past the bench, hand-in-hand.

He stopped and Sarah slipped her hand free.

"Daddy, can I play in the sand box?"

"Sure, but stay where I can see you."

Blonde braids bobbed as she skipped.

He waited until she settled in the box, then asked, "Mind if I join you?"

"Not at all." Jan dumped her backpack to the ground.

Seated at an angle allowed him to face Jan and keep an eye on his daughter. "Thank you again for stopping her. Sarah gets so excited sometimes. I have a hard time keeping up with her."

"I don't have any kids." Why'd she say that? "Um, I mean I…"

He glanced at her sketchpad. "You sure know how to draw them. Who's the little girl?"

As he pointed to the picture—a girl in full pump, hair flying, cares forgotten—Jan noticed no wedding ring.

"No one in particular. She's the embodiment of all kids who thrill at the motion of the swing."

"I see that. Makes me want to jump on a swing." His warm laugh washed over her.

Imagine him flying through the air.

Again he pointed to the pad in her lap. "Why are you sketching kids on swings?"

What should she say? Option one: he was merely being polite because she'd helped his daughter. Or, option two: he had a genuine interest. She preferred the latter and decided to share her passion. "I illustrate children's books and I'm presently working on one titled *The Playground Adventure*. The author wants old-fashioned paintings, not computer generated pictures. The proofs are due next week."

"No kidding. What books have you illustrated?"

Jan named a few. "But my favorite is the *Mr. Caterpillar* series written by Pete Andrews."

"I've heard of him. In fact my sister recommended I purchase his books for Sarah's birthday. I'll have to check out *Mr. Caterpillar*."

"There are five in the set. I consider them my best work."

"A book illustrator. I've never met one before."

"I also paint landscapes, portraits. I have space in a gallery downtown." She barreled full speed along the road for option two.

"That's interesting—" His phone beeped. He nabbed it from his pocket and viewed the screen. "Sorry, I have to take this." Stepping a few feet away, he conversed in a low tone.

Jan flipped the page and searched the playground for another subject.

When Sarah's father returned to the bench, a frown creased his brow. "Sarah and I need to leave." He withdrew a thin silver case from his back pocket and extracted a card. "Here's my business card. If ever you need my help, please give me a call." His fingers lingered on the yellow and blue card as Jan reached for it. His gaze raked her face for a moment before he let go.

"Thank you." She scanned the print. *KJ Hatcher, MA; MEd. Licensed Professional Counselor. Specializing in Christian based Principles.* Did he think she needed his services? Before she could voice her question, he strode to the sandbox and took Sarah's hand. They crossed the playground and zigzagged through the parking lot.

Jan gave his card another peek. *KJ* What did the initials stand for? She noted his office was close by. Did he really think she needed someone to talk to, or was his gesture merely a sincere *thank you*? She slipped the card into her pocket and pursed her lips. Although she'd enjoyed the father-daughter interlude, she wondered if the anxiety brought on by the phone call showed on her face.

Giving herself a mental shake, Jan settled her sketchpad firmly on her lap. But her pencil lay idle. For the most part, her life since Bradley's disappearance satisfied her. Volunteer work at the children's shelter, the company of her sisters and friends from university, and her rewarding career as an independent artist filled her time. Then why did the simple act of keeping a stranger's child from danger emphasize the void in her life?

The *what if* game came calling. What if she had a little girl who liked to run at the park? What if Bradley hadn't left? Her mood darkened along with the sky.

Children's laughter interrupted her daydream. She rubbed her cold hands together. If only she could warm her heart as easily. Focused again on the swings in front of her where two young boys were trying to swing in rhythm, she straightened the pad on her lap. Pencil in hand she sketched their body movements, reveling in the skritching of lead on parchment.

A cold wind stirred the dead leaves under the bench. Fat drops of water splattered on her sketchpad. Screaming children and yelling parents announced the rain's arrival. With a groan, Jan snatched up her backpack, rammed the pad in, and raced to her car. Completing the sketches had to wait.

The drive home wouldn't take long, but Jan dreaded spending the evening alone. She'd been fine until the phone call which gnawed at her gut. Until the threat, she'd believed Bradley left because he didn't want to marry her, but now the caller hinted at a more sinister reason. Turning left at the light, she stopped at her favorite pizza parlor, and after ordering, called Delany, her middle sister. Busy studying for a major exam, Del declined in the invitation.

Disappointment covered Jan like a metal shawl. She'd eat alone in her big house. With an ache growing in her heart, she paid for the pizza. Savory aromas of cheese, pepperoni, and peppers exuded from the box as it warmed her hands.

The rain had stopped. Streetlights glistened off the wet tarmac, and people huddled into their coats as they hurried along. Jan climbed into her car. She shivered as she drove through the neighborhood. More than the outside temperature chilled her to the core.

She gave up her feeble attempts to be nonchalant. Maybe it was the rain that finally got to her.

It had also rained the day Bradley left.

Loss engulfed her, sapping every ounce of life out of her body. She concentrated on her driving as she followed the familiar route home. Stopped at a traffic light, she glanced at the dark sedan in the next lane. The driver leered at her but quickly turned to his companion. When the light changed, Jan thought nothing more about the incident as the car zoomed ahead.

Thick, dark clouds brought on an early dusk. Jan turned down her street and an on-coming vehicle's high beams blinded her. Blinking, she hugged the right side of the road, but the car careened straight for her. Jan honked and flashed her lights. The car kept coming, now just yards away. Heat surged up from her boots, her breath came in short gulps. Her hands ached gripping the wheel. Parked cars lined the street. She couldn't escape. The lights were mere feet away. She braced for impact, but the car veered and skimmed by her. It screeched around the corner and disappeared.

Her driveway beckoned and Jan roared into it. Pressing the remote with quivering fingers, she drove into her garage, quickly closed the door and sat in the car, glued to the seat. Was that the same vehicle she'd seen earlier? The seed of fear sprouted roots that forced their way through Jan's body. Blood pounded like thundering ocean waves in her head.

A sliver of sanity admonished her. "You can't sit out here all night." She sucked in a breath, balanced the pizza box on her backpack and scurried inside, setting the alarm system before dumping everything on the kitchen table. As she hung up her jacket, her cell phone rang. She glared at the screen.

Another number without a name. The same one? She couldn't remember.

In no emotional state to suffer more harassment, she allowed the call to go to voicemail.

Jan sank onto a chair and waited for the message beep.

Tapping the icon with a shaking index finger, she held her breath.

"Where'd you learn to drive like that?" Not the same voice as before. "Next time we meet, you'd better tell me what I want to know."

Her nails dug into her palms as she pounded her fists on the table. "What do you want?"

www.ingramcontent.com/pod-product-compliance
Lightning Source LLC
Chambersburg PA
CBHW061017120726
47910CB00006B/1986